PIRATE JENNY

PIRATE JENNY

BY APRIL BERNARD

W · W · Norton & Company
New York · London

Printed in the United States of America.

Lyrics by Bertolt Brecht, copyright Suhrkamp Verlag.

English translation of *The Threepenny Opera* by Marc Blitzstein, copyright Warner/Chappell Music.

The text of this book is composed in Baskerville.
Composition and manufacturing by the Haddon Craftsmen Inc.
Book design by Guenet Abraham.

First Edition

Library of Congress Cataloging-in-Publication Data
Bernard, April.
    Pirate Jenny / by April Bernard.
        p. cm.

ISBN 0-393-02821-6

    I. Title.
    PS3552.E7258P5 1990
    813'.54—dc20   89-35319

W. W. Norton & Company, Inc., 500 Fifth Avenue,
New York, N. Y. 10110

W. W. Norton & Company, Ltd., 37 Great Russell Street,
London WC1B 3NU

1 2 3 4 5 6 7 8 9 0

Grateful acknowledgment is made to Luc Sante; to Claire and Walter Bernard; to my agent, Eric Ashworth, and my editor, Hilary Hinzmann; and to all the friends whose advice and assistance has been so helpful—especially Sara Driver, Michael Shulan, and Duncan Stalker.

FOR MY SISTER, LISA BERNARD

PIRATE JENNY

1

THE ROOT BEER BARN WHERE CONNIE
Frances LaPlante (called Jenny) worked that summer had
been open for more than ten years under different manage-
ments. First there had been the reign of Uncle Sammy
Chenowski, who had dressed the carhops in the company's
top-of-the-line outfits, orange scalloped minis that looked
like skating costumes. Jenny had been a very little girl then.
A drive alone with the Dads to the Root Beer Barn was a
high and solemn occasion. While the Dads joked with the
carhop, his daughter listened, concentrating on his every
turn of the head, the way he'd dissolve a laugh into a cough
before it went on too long. And she longed for him to shine
his face on her and laugh the way he did at home: *"Who's*

my little Con? *You?* No, you're way too grown-up. Where's my little baby girl?"—looking behind the couch, falling on all fours and checking under the tables, while she giggled and screamed, "Me, me, me, me, me!"

The metal tray would be fixed to the rolled-down window, the enormous dimpled glass mugs would arrive half filled with sticky beige foam. When the Dads looked, Jenny would remember to smile at him as she put the mug back on the tray, two-handed so as not to spill; then laboriously, kneeling on the seat, take it back in both hands for the next sip on the straw. She never, never spilled.

Successive owners came and went; carhops went completely out of fashion, even in Chester. But George, the newest owner, a slick from a college town about fifty miles away, dismantled the speaker at the drive-through window, found a shiny, salmony-orange paint for the building, and reinstated carhopping. He said it was hip.

"It's hip, kiddo. Everything old is new again, you know?" He tugged Jenny's ponytail. "Right, kiddo?"

The current generation of Root Beer Barn girls wore ponytails or pigtails, black T-shirts and white short-shorts with orange suspenders on which black and orange "How May I Serve U?" and "Cold 'n' Frosty" buttons were affixed.

That late June day, nothing much was going on. The new office phone was being installed, so George spent most of his day out on the lot, talking into the pay phone about some deal he wanted to swing over the line in Cummington County, something about buying an abandoned drive-in movie lot. The girls giggled about it—in a proprietary way, since after all George was beefy and blond and dressed sort of beach-bum cute and had some money. He was their main topic of conversation at work, and a couple of the girls tossed their ponytails and teased him: "Take me to the drive-in, Georgie!" "How many can you stuff in the backseat?"

Jenny envisioned a cartoon version of dozens of ponytails flying out the windows and trunk of the car while the pasha George honked his horn. She started to roll her eyes, then stopped. She was remembering not to roll her eyes.

The driver of the blue Japanese van looked down at the top of her head when she took his order. She appeared to be studying his tires. Her hair, brown with chemical gold streaks, was piled in a kewpie-doll topknot. Her sallow skin resisted tan, and a series of sunburnt flushes mottled her legs. When she brought his root beer, her plain, sharp features pointed off at the horizon; but despite her apparent inattention, she did not spill. Only when she brought him the check did Jenny hand him her smile, too: a broad flash with plenty of teeth, ferocious, astonishing in its insincerity, or maybe she really meant it after all? The tip was, as usual, excessive.

At four-thirty, Jenny's shift was done. She changed in the bathroom, into halter top and long tight plaid shorts—one of her experiments, a twenty-five-cent yard-sale trophy. She kept the white visor on her head, but stuffed her other work clothes into a vinyl bag.

Route 9 ran through Chester, that town's only real highway. The Root Beer Barn inhabited a lot on the shopping strip east of town, and Jenny lived about a twenty-minute walk west of there. Chester was a mill town, on the Blue River; in the last century, three lumber mills and a tannery crowded along one five-mile stretch of the river, where the water ran narrow and swift. Now the mills and the big shots who owned them had gone; only one paper mill remained, where the tannery used to be. The Blue River had been renamed the Pattatuck River fifty years ago by the state, in a fit of authenticity inspired by the centennial of something or other. Likewise the Patty Mountains, north of town. Oddly enough, the name change coincided almost exactly with the introduction of synthetic dyes at the mill—but even as the river became a murky smelly rainbow of purples, greens, yellows, and pinks, the residents of Chester stuck to calling their river Blue.

Right where the highway went past the mill, the edge of the hills pushed the road almost into the river, and the roar of the water was loud in Jenny's ears as she walked by. She never noticed the noise except that one time, years ago, when she *couldn't* hear it. The Dads had gotten a job in the mill for a few months and she had gone to bring him his lunch. The noise inside the mill was so great that it drowned out the river: huge swaying rolls that fed the wet paper up to the ceiling and back down, carousels of stacked napkins tipped and straightened and then diapered with brown wrappers, all thumping and banging in such a tumult of noise that she had started to scream, but there was no sound, so it was like screaming in a dream.

Gigantic uncut rolls of colored paper sat in the gravel yard outside the mill, under corrugated plastic sheds and sheets of blue plastic. Gray metal semis emblazoned with the CHESTER PAPERS logo jackknifed gingerly onto the highway, swaying with loads of boxes of pink and blue and white toilet paper, improbably heraldic paper towels, and damask-textured dinner napkins. As Jenny walked by the link fence of the mill, she waved to one of the drivers, a sometime boyfriend of her mother's whom she called Fat-but-Fast. He beeped.

The river was yellow that day, a churning lemonade over

III PIRATE JENNY III

the rocks, thick canary-yellow in the little pools next to the shore. Jenny walked downstream along the highway, then turned by habit a few steps to the water and fished up a bit of white quartz well stained with yellow. Like nearly every other child in town, she had a shoe-box collection of dyed rocks at home. But she was too old for that now, so she dropped it and went on.

Crossing Route 9, she detoured to the SuperSave. The new asphalt on the parking lot gave off the kind of tough chemical smell Jenny respected. She paused to breathe it in, admiring the black lava that had been poured even farther than usual at the edges, lapping the trunks of the trash trees, sumac and poplar, that ringed the lot. In the express lane, Jenny paid for a carton of low-tar cigarettes, cranberry juice, a couple of cantaloupes, and, as an afterthought, a tabloid with a good picture and cover story: "The Bear That Plays Chess—And Stumps the Experts!" With white plastic shopping bag in one hand and white vinyl carryall in the other, she trudged homeward up Kenney's Road behind SuperSave—a skinny, plaid-knickered pack mule.

When Jenny saw the note on the kitchen table, in familiar handwriting, she swiftly reached for the handle of the fridge. As expected: the beer was gone. She squatted down to the cupboard beneath the sink. Everything gone but a half-empty bottle of bourbon, which the Dads never drank anyway.

She dropped her groceries on the table, sat down heavily, and read the note.

Dear Kitten,
I borrowed some beer. You can come to this party tonight if you want—I know you would like

Linda but I understand if you would prefer to run around with one of your many gentleman friends. Tell the Con I miss her.

Best,
F.

Five years of disorganized noncohabitation had not diminished Frank's freedom to move in and out of his former home. Though Jenny composed her face into a semblance of patience to listen, often, to Kitten's laments, she was secretly on her father's side. She loved his maneuvers around her mother, his emotional sleight-of-hand: buy a little stuffed koala teddy bear (Kitten loved teddy bears), or a little yellow kitten (who was now a big fat cat), spend the night, borrow fifty dollars in the morning, and disappear for a couple of months. Though despising her mother as a pushover, Jenny habitually snubbed her father to his face; her admiration, and her longing, were safely quiet. He would smile that heart-breaker smile: "How's my Con?" But her smile identical to his, her twin boat with a dimple wake on one side, would not sail. Instead her lips stayed puffed, inert, purplish, in the repose that was like a permanent sneer: "Fine."

She had learned it all from him. He used to say, "The con is the best, the tops, he's the primo artisto, honey pie. You know a great dancer, like Fred Astaire? They always say, 'He makes it look so easy.' But old Fred, he's got the fatal weakness, he still needs the applause. A con don't make it look *easy*. A con don't make it *look at all*. Inside," he pointed to the cracked belt at his thin waist, "that's the only place you hear the cheering." He looked very serious. "This takes discipline. You're always onstage, but only you know

▌▌▌ P I R A T E J E N N Y ▌▌▌

it. It is," he opened his pale grey eyes, held his daughter's head between his hands, and whispered, "Zen."

And to Jenny, that need, her own dreadful hunger, was forever misnamed. Why did she want the aqua mohair sweater that the girl in her chem class wore—so badly that she spilled a bottle of Bromine on it and they had to evacuate the whole room from the fumes? Why did she angle for weeks to get the Dumar twins to invite her to ride between them in their black convertible Mustang, only to rage silently on that afternoon as she sailed down the strip, because the smaller boy sucked on his cola and rubbed his knee on hers? Why did she clench her teeth and stare at the long heavy furs draped over tall blonde Czechoslovakian bodies in the fashion magazines, who were otherwise clad only in shimmering teddies and stockings held up by white fur pom-pom garters?

Why, since the age of six, had she kept her eyes shut after waking in the morning, wishing for the movie to begin, willing that there be pink satin sheets and long velvet curtains and a built-in bar, a vanity table strewn with silver and crystal, a black-haired French woman in an apron who would come bustling through the door with a huge silver breakfast tray? Silver coffeepot, silver toast rack, and also a golden tiara she could put in her hair? And why would the curtains be flung open to reveal a tall splendid shining city outside, with taxis and tuxedos and mustaches and champagne? Jenny opened her eyes to dark brown paneling that echoed when you bumped your head, the scorched paper lampshade where Cinderella chatted with a blue birdie perched on her finger, and the brown paisley curtains hanging as a door to the clothes closet.

Why did she feel the longing and curl tight in a ball under the covers? She muttered the wrong word: "Zen."

JENNY WAS PAGING RESTLESSLY THROUGH A BACK NUMBER OF A fashion magazine when Kitten came home. The spring lock in the front door wheezed and squealed and then slammed without locking, like a violent sneeze.

"Hi, baby, how's the Con?"

"Yeah. Fine. Behold your cigarettes."

"Thanks, baby. God! What a rotten stinkeroo of a day, start to . . . Shit!" She saw Frank's note. "What's he done now?"

Jenny rose, letting the magazine slide off her lap onto the rug, and jammed her visor back on. "Got to go to the library." She pushed the wheezing door. "It's open late tonight." She was down the steps.

"Con? Connie?" The daughter turned and stared blankly at the mother, the sun full on her pale hazel eyes. Kitten held the long, limp cat to her cheek and waved the note like a flag in the other hand. "Don't forget," she called, "look for the jazzercise and *Sins of the Sons*?"

"Right."

The library was a quarter mile west of SuperSave, in what had once been the center of town. The lumber fortunes had joined in a white clapboard lineup, five houses on either side of the main road, with lawns that crept back like hoisted skirts when Route 9 was widened. One had been turned into the town hall, and two others were linked by a walkway into the local professional building, housing a lawyer, a realtor, two accountants, and a dental practice.

Closer to the road and in their midst sat the big white Congregational Church, with its spindly bell-tower spire.

⫼ PIRATE JENNY ⫼

No one rang the bell anymore: on Sundays recorded chimes clicked on at eight and noon, beckoning the parishioners with a tinny noise that quickly dissipated in the air.

Kitten still went to church sometimes, but she belonged to St. Catherine's RC, a small stone heap set on a side street down by the river for the Poles and the French Canadians. When she was very small, wedged down on the kneeler between her parents, Jenny would hallucinate heaven by staring into the green glass of a fifty-cent ring. It came from a coin-op machine at the grocery store, in one of those plastic eggs that usually contained nothing more glamorous than a black rubber scorpion or a small pink plastic doll. But the green ring, Jenny's emerald, was grand enough to take to church. While Kitten buried her head (onto which a square of white lace was fixed with a bobby pin) in her hands and the Dads half kneeled, half sat against the pew, Jenny stared into the green facets of her ring, catching the reflections from the stained glass tableaux in the windows: Joseph in a yellow-brown coat, beneath a weeping willow tree; Mary in blue with a herd of white lambs at her feet and a white dove sitting on her shoulder; St. Bartholomew, with a knife and a long dark beard. When the glass in the ring got loose, Jenny could spin it and make the saints spin, too, like a merry-go-round, or a wheeling rose. These days everyone said St. Catherine's was sinking into the bog, and surveyors hired by the diocese had come by in the spring and shaken their heads and suggested a fund drive.

Past the Congregational, the Earliest House, dated 1767 on the doorframe, had been turned into the town library. Jenny put her feet into the shallow trough steps of worn marble and leaned on the new maple door, which stuck. Her breath always got short when she approached this scene of many small crimes. From the age of eight, she'd been stealing novels from the shelves and storing them in her closet at home. She had acquired quite a range from the Penguin classics paperbacks; she especially liked Dickens, though she was usually too engrossed by the maddening suspense as the characters churned about in their pride and conceit and honor to look up the words she didn't understand. A double edition of *Dracula* and *Frankenstein* looked very exciting, but the stories were disappointingly slow, like wading in dark muddy puddles; Jenny had seen a *Dracula* television movie that she liked much better. But she kept the book, as she kept all the others. She liked having them in her closet. And of course there were all those romance novels, the paperbacks with the fair-haired girl running in wisps of gauze from a dark house, her eyes rolled wildly to one side as the shadowy figure of a man loomed in her wake. These bored Jenny quickly, but she was easily seduced anew by a variation on the cover. What if the girl was running from a cliff? From a lighthouse? What if the menacing shadow seemed female? Or the girl's garments looked Spanish? What if she clutched in her hand a bloody knife? Jenny would want to know every time, and she'd tuck the paperback under her shirt and nurse it there on the way home.

These days she avoided novels altogether. She walked into the record room and pretended to browse for a while, flipping through the familiar heavy boxed sets of operas, the piano études, the London Symphony collections of Popular Favorites. The plastic sheaths slapped against each other as she checked out the rest of the room. No one was looking. She selected "Romantic Greats: Nocturnes of Chopin."

In the foreign bin, she found the new two-record set of

The Threepenny Opera, a different recording from the one she already had at home. She froze for a moment, counting to twenty. Then swiftly she slid one record out of the jacket and tucked it into the sleeve next to the nocturnes. Now she was safe, she could pause for a minute to study the album art on *The Threepenny Opera:* a hideous clownish face, winking beneath a bowler; a stage banked with fog across which a line of women stalked on tiptoe; a man slapping a woman, her back to the audience; her face tilted almost full around by the force of the blow; a man and a woman embracing while other men leered. Taking up another record at random, a collection of Irish folk songs, she slid the other disc of the opera into that sleeve.

Now that the first part of the job was done, Jenny moved from the room with a brisk, even officious, air. Visitors to the library often mistook her for one of Mrs. Feehan's girls. Sometimes Jenny sternly delivered random directions in answer to their queries: "Last shelf, high, on the left." When she took the Chopin and the Irish songs to the front desk, she observed that Mrs. Feehan was in one of her moods. Tactfully, Jenny did not venture the smile, merely said a meek "Thank you" as Mrs. Feehan stamped the cards and left, holding her treasures casually, letting them slide about in her hands like things of no consequence.

Since Kitten LaPlante's house, at the top of Kenney's Road, sat on the last bit of hillside before it got too steep to build on, the house had only half a storey downstairs. Jenny's bedroom upstairs was the one that faced the hill, her window looking right out level with the tree roots. There was no one to see in but the birds and the squirrels and the occasional cat. But Jenny closed her bedroom curtains, yanking the heavy paisley seized in the jaws of gilt café-curtain rings. She took the stolen records out and carefully put the first one on her stereo. The other she added to the pile on the bookshelf, all of them neatly stacked between squares of wax paper, like so many pieces of ham: *Johnny Johnson, The Seven Deadly Sins, Lady in the Dark,* "Berlin Cabaret Songs," *Mahagonny, Die Dreigroschenoper, Happy End.*

Jenny had never stolen a record when she picked up *The Threepenny Opera* from the library, in the fall of the previous year, enticed by the sinful looks of the striped skirts and rouged faces on the cover. It was too big to hide under her jacket, so she had actually checked it out at the desk. The music staggered her. It was like absolutely nothing she had ever heard before—a raggedy, wild sound that went deep inside. The dark minor keys, the story of the evil hero, Macheath the killer, who wins in the end; all the dark, fast ballads advertising a life of theft and agility. Most of all, Lotte Lenya's trembling voice, tart as a green apple, filled her with such passionate recognition, that when she heard "Pirate Jenny" for the first time, she stood bolt upright and waved rigid hands in front of her, as if warding something away. The song called to a black revenge in her own soul: the scrub girl Jenny dreams of a pirate ship that will sail her into the harbor, cannons booming, to save her from the degradations of her sorry life, slaughter her tormentors, crown her the true Pirate Queen, and sail her away to glory.

When the Dads had left them that first time, Kitten had scrambled for a job, and wound up for a time as a housekeeper, cleaning the big white manses in town, and the new ritzy ranch houses up in the hills. Some afternoons Jenny had gone along to help. She learned that silver needs to be polished, that rich people keep shabby family snapshots in elegant frames, that glasses from the dishwasher must be polished for spots before they go into the cupboard, that gentlemen get spray starch on their collars and cuffs, that fancy soap is shaped like shells and flowers and is replaced every week, that proper tablecloths and napkins are made of heavy ivory linen that must be ironed but not burned, that the things in the drawer in the sideboard were not small bracelets but napkin rings.

So she knew all about what Pirate Jenny wished:

> *You gentlemen can watch while I'm scrubbin the floors*
> *And I'm scrubbin the floors while you're gawkin*
> *And maybe once you tip me and it makes you feel swell*
> *On a ratty waterfront, in a ratty old hotel*
> *And you never guess to who you're talkin*
> *You never guess to who you're talkin. . . .*
>
> *And a ship, a black freighter*
> *With a skull on its masthead*
> *Will be comin in. . . .*
>
> *But I'm countin your heads while I make up the beds*
> *'Cause there's nobody gonna sleep here;*
> *Tonight, none of you will sleep here. . . .*
>
> *And the ship, the black freighter,*
> *Turns around in the harbor,*
> *Shootin guns from the bow. . . .*
>
> *And they're chainin up people and bringin em to me,*
> *Askin me, "Kill em now, or later?"*
> *Askin me, "Kill em now, or later?"*
>   *Noon by the clock, and so still on the dock*
> *You can hear a foghorn miles away—*
> *In that quiet of death I'll say, "Right now."*
> *And they'll pile up the bodies and I'll say,*
> *"That'll learn ya."*

And the ship, the black freighter,
Disappears out to sea
And on it is me.

That was when she changed her name, of course. At school she explained it to her guidance counselor by saying that she had just learned who Connie Francis was, and she was ashamed to be named after an old singer. Jenny had only two girlfriends of any intimacy; Karen told her it wasn't legal to change your name. Jenny explained that Connie was a nickname, that her birth certificate actually said Jenny. Then Ellen got so excited that for a while she said *she* was Connie now, but everyone made fun of her so she quit it.

Meanwhile, the record was long overdue, but Jenny couldn't bear to return it. One evening when Frank came by and Kitten was out, Jenny nervously put the needle on the disc so he could hear the song Mr. Peachum sings:

If first you don't succeed,
Then try and try again,
And if you don't succeed again,
Just try and try and try.
Useless, it's useless, our kind of life's too tough.
Take it from me, it's useless;
Trying ain't enough.

But he drank a beer and kept talking over the music. He showed his daughter a new card trick. He told her to mark a card with a crayon, then he put it back into the deck and shuffled it. He threw the deck in the air, stuck out a saucer, and caught the right card from the fluttering rain. She had drawn a skull and crossbones, but he didn't notice.

III PIRATE JENNY III

"Dads, this one is great, you'll really like this one!" She jumped the needle to a song of the hero's good advice:

> *Where's the percentage?*
> *Ask Mack the Knife.*
> *The bulging pocket makes the easy life.*

But her father only listened to the first verse before he wandered into the kitchen and lit a joint. "Kraut music," he said knowingly. "Ja, ja, ja, ja!" he shouted the notes of the drinking song and swung his beer glass up towards the ceiling. "Drink to me only with thine eye-eyes, and I-I will drink to thee!" He hopped a little soft-shoe routine. "Hey!" he shouted. "This guy I know, he's a theatrical agent, says I've got that all-around quality of a real performer. And I says, 'What's it to me?' And he says, 'No, you should go on the stage!' What do you think, Connie? Don't you bet the camera would love this face?"

Jenny took the record off the turntable. "My name is Jenny," she said, and left the room.

"Bullshit!" her father shouted. "Your name is Sauerkraut!"

Jenny went upstairs and shut the door. She did not come back down when Frank left a half hour later, but sat and stared at the album cover and then played the opera again, singing along. All the songs seemed even more private than before. They were not sung to the other characters but to the audience, and the audience was only Jenny listening alone in the darkening room: "Here's my point of view! Here's my story, my life, my philosophy. We can act a different way when there are other people around, but here in this private moment, just between you and me and the litter box, we know the real story. Life sucks, but you can still get a good deal if you're sharp." There was such promise, such dark hope, and everything just around the corner!

As Jenny sang, she brooded on her father, who seemed almost—well, he was—pathetic. Where was his famous discipline? The movies. Right. His pocket did not bulge with cash; no one feared him or bowed to him in the street. He was king of nothing. She sat up all night, sneering.

Finally the library sent notes and called. Jenny took her mother with her to pay them off, claiming she had lost the record. With the twelve-dollar fine, the library got a new copy of the same record a few weeks later. Jenny switched discs, acquiring the new, unscratched one for herself. After that she began stealing other records of music by Kurt Weill and with singing by Lotte Lenya—and Grete Keller, who sounded so sweet, and Marlene Dietrich. Dietrich had a funny drawling way of singing, and Jenny played "See What the Boys in the Back Room Will Have," and "Falling in Love Again." But she liked Lenya's voice the best. She hated to leave the covers behind in the record room, but *Mahagonny* had a loose booklet with lyrics and translations, and the big Lotte Lenya album had pictures and a biography, and she kept those. At Christmas her father gave her a cassette machine, and she taped them all. But she loved the discs too much to return them to the library. And almost as much as she loved having them, she loved no one else having them.

She was intoxicated with the sound of the German, the way it hissed and guttered in the mouth, so much fiercer than the English translations:

> *Denn wie man sicht bettet, so licht man*
> *Es decht einen keiner das zu.*
> *Und wenn einer getrittet, dann bin ich es.*
> *Und wird einer getreten, dann bist du.*

III   PIRATE JENNY   III

It sounded like animals, like something from inside her growling and moaning and laughing and escaping as music. In *Mahagonny,* everyone said "whiskey" with a couple of extra esses in the middle, like thirsty snakes. Jenny began sneaking drinks from her mother's bottle, even though she had never liked the burning taste of bourbon. "Is there no whisssssskey in this town?" she would sing, mournfully.

She discovered that there were many Jennys—the loose and slangy Jenny of *Mahagonny,* the simpering Jenny of *Down in the Valley.* Jenny knew she was the girl "who would make up her mind" from the "Saga of Jenny" in *Lady in the Dark,* but most of all she was Pirate Jenny Diver, bitter and broken-hearted but with those stirring bloody dreams. She sang along with Lenya, imitating her crippled English:

> *"An ya see me kinda starin out the winda*
> *An ya wonda, 'What's she got ta stare at now?'"*

Or in German, on the "Barbara Song," which tells the story of a girl who was brought up to say NO, but then one day a man comes along who doesn't give her time, so how could she say it then, the fruitless *Nein* croaked in a descending tremolo, like some terrible lost bird.

THAT NIGHT, AFTER HER MOTHER WENT OUT, JENNY LISTENED to her new version of *The Threepenny Opera*—it was a different English translation, and the songs went on longer, and there was more of a circus-oompah-band sound. All alone in her bedroom Jenny sang and danced, pounded her feet and waved her arms above her head, jumped on the bed and on the floor, triumphant, determined, scaring herself with her own rage. Tonight the songs sounded like marches, thump, thump, to battle, while the melody slid around on a slinky clarinet or a steel-stringed guitar, mocking the battle. What did it matter where these songs came from, who Weill was or who Lenya? History is dead, Jenny thought, and she believed the thought was new. She took the music into her and remade it there. Finally, all the songs were about her. They were her marching anthems, into what battle she was not sure, but she would march and secretly laugh at the marching, she would fight and scorn the blood that was shed.

Much later at night, when Kitten was in bed asleep, Jenny plugged in her earphones and sang along, softly:

> *Remember wise old Solomon,*
> *Recall his history—*
> *He was the wisest man on earth,*
> *And so he cursed the day of his birth. . . .*

2

MARKIE LEANED OUT OF HIS BROTHER'S
jeep. "After you're done work?"

Jenny regarded him stony-faced. "Since you ask so nice."

The jeep chugged and departed with a spew of gravel.
Val said loudly to the other girls, "That his own wheels?"

Jenny glared at them, retrieved her new sunglasses from
their perch on her hair, and slid them down on her face.
They were round, like a blind man's glasses, only silver-
coated. The girls giggled.

It was a preposterously hot July day, with the kind of heat
that assaults from all sides: great ripples of black heat from
the asphalt, a steady hammer of white heat from the sun—
and when the wind blew, that was the hottest of all. It was

much too hot for root beer. Only one car stopped in two hours. The driver rolled her window down just a crack when she ordered, and quickly handed the tray back when it came, taking her food in the car.

Under the awning, George leaned across the counter and rubbed a cold mug against the back of Jenny's neck.

"Hey, you want to come sit in my office a minute, kiddo? You look ready to die."

Jenny walked into the air conditioning, and for a moment felt almost sick from relief, as if she'd fallen into an ice-water bath and couldn't shiver. She turned to George as he shut the door, took off her shades, and smiled.

"So," he said, "Markie's your boyfriend?"

"From time to time," she said, brushing her hand along the desk and wishing she was wearing pale blue satin, and nibbling on a cigarette holder. Where could she find a cigarette holder? An antique store, maybe. She sat down in George's desk chair and pulled her knees up to her chin, hugging them.

"Isn't he a little old for you?"

Jenny laughed her new laugh, the short silver-bells one. "A May-June romance? Pretty racy. He's only a year older than you."

George actually batted his blond lashes. "How do you know how old I am?"

This was purposeless. Jenny reached over and switched on the radio. Soupy pop music seeped in under the rhythmic roar of the air conditioner. She turned it off.

"So—you're going into the movie business?"

"Maybe. A drive-in."

"You should get Markie to manage it, or something."

"Would you like that? Well, sure, maybe. Tell him to give me a call."

Jenny looked straight into George's pale goofy eyes and whispered, "Thanks, kiddo." She got up, and, in a gesture much practiced before the bathroom mirror, stretched her arms over her head, baring a white midriff. She paused just a moment too long, and George laughed. Unblinking, and glad that she no longer blushed, she strolled out of the office.

In the evening, on the way to the dump, Jenny studied the dark hair on Markie's arm critically. "Think you could operate a drive-in?" she asked.

"A what?"

Enunciating clearly, slowly: "A drive-in movie theater. George is buying an old one. Says you should call him."

"You think you're my career counselor?"

Jenny stared at his arm. "Have you considered shaving your arms?"

"Something's wrong with you today, doll face."

"That's a dumb expression, cheese ball."

"Doll face."

"Have you ever been to the Cummington Flea Market?" she asked suddenly. They had things like cigarette holders at flea markets. Markie ignored her and pulled his sticky shirt away from the seat back.

"Drive-in movies! Jesus." He hunched his bulk over the steering column and frowned at the road. "This weekend, anyway, I decided. It's the Navy. That's it."

"You crave the salt air."

"Absolutely. Dan and me went to camp summers on the Cape. Sailing, deep-sea fishing, it's the best." It was a speech. "And it means money and all those career-training perks and I'm already in great shape so training'll be—easy as jello."

"I hear the Navy makes you shave your whole body, including your arms."

He looked over and saw the smile. "Shit, you're a pain in the tail." He squeezed her knee. His smile, a crooked one between bumpy lips, was dark and rare—it seemed yanked out of him. It was aimed at the road, but Jenny saw it, and drew in her breath—then to cover the sound, she slapped his hand away.

Frogpond Road dead-ended at the landfill. In the heat, the crows were only half pretending to care about the garbage. They perched on the dead swamp-tree tops cawing intermittently, or languidly shaking out their wings.

Two cars and a pickup were parked around the shack where the dump manager sat every day, inhaling the waste and checking out permit stickers on the bumpers of the cars and sorting the colored glass in the recycling shed. Eddie Feehan was the new dump manager, and he had already made a name for himself. Just after Thanksgiving, he had stuffed a discarded pink metal Christmas tree into the mound of snow next to his shack and decorated it with assorted detritus—white plastic bleach bottles, sneakers, broken dolls, plastic spoons. A photo of Eddie grinning next to his tree appeared in the local paper and was picked up by a national wire service.

Chester was proud of Eddie, as it was proud of its dump—having waged a five-year campaign in the state legislature for their very own landfill, so they wouldn't have to keep trucking their garbage twenty miles away to Hudson. Local enthusiasts had printed up bumper stickers that read "Chester Dump for Chester Residents." Of course, that made the kids fall all over themselves. Because of his tree, Eddie, only a year out of high school himself, became a kind of mascot. The kids persuaded him to leave the tree up once the winter passed. That spring and summer, the dump became their place to gather.

III   PIRATE JENNY   III

As usual, the kids drank beer and coolers and passed the joints. Marquette and Deboise and Krullmeyer had a throwing contest, shying bottles and stones into the marsh, calling on the girls to judge size of splash. Only Debbie, listlessly, umped: "That's one for Deboise. . . . Tie, Deboise and Markie. . . . Another *big* one for Deboise. . . ."

Corey, Debbie D., and Shawn sat on the bed of Eddie's truck and talked shop—deodorants and quick-tan, the latter of which they agreed only worked on the legs, and only if someone else smeared it on. They touched upon the central source of local dismay: that the new clothing store in the Hudson mall had those long heavy plastic tags on all the clothes. Shoplifting would soon be impossible everywhere—that was the dire prediction. Shawn said her cousin said that the grocery stores would be doing the same thing, some sort of device that glowed in the dark, like X-ray machines at the airport. Jenny decided to keep to herself the information recently acquired from the Dads, that if you wrapped the plastic tag in aluminum foil, the detector didn't pick it up. She had yet to test it, but that wasn't why she didn't share the news.

Ellen, who was in a major mood from boyfriend troubles and brother troubles and teacher troubles and some half-baked story about the Mafia being after her uncle, sat in the front seat of Krullmeyer's pickup, playing the radio and hogging a dime bag. She had taken to wearing all black this summer, a black tank shirt and black jeans greying with dirt, but she had very long nails that were coated with several layers of tangerine lacquer, which Jenny very much admired.

"So Ellen," she said. "Can you show me how to put on those fake nails?" She displayed her own frayed finger ends. "I can't stop biting mine."

"You need a kit," said Ellen, not offering her the joint. "Costs more than seven dollars. Why don't you just stop biting them?"

Jenny contemplated the mascara circles under Ellen's eyes. "Someone been abusing you?" she asked sarcastically. "Got a couple of black eyes there."

Ellen looked at herself in the rearview mirror and hastily smudged the circles away. "Shut up," she said.

A crow shook his wing, flicked it, as if he had a piece of plastic tape stuck in his feathers. Jenny laughed, and then saw that Eddie was watching her. "That's Rosalie," he explained. He told her the names of all the crows that ringed the trees overhead, and who was married to whom, and what their jobs were. One was an accountant. Jenny offered Eddie one of her hair clips, a red plastic star, for the top of his tree. She wondered what his reaction would be, but hadn't expected to see his eyes fill with tears. It was embarrassing.

A couple of hours later, when a few more kids had pulled up and Krullmeyer and Debbie D. had driven away—her parents were away camping—everyone decided to go to the Tubs, a swimming spot about ten miles upstream on the Blue, where centuries of waterfalls had made a series of basins in the rock. The caravan of cars and bikes and trucks lurched up Frogpond, and onto the back road that ran parallel to the river.

Carl, Krullmeyer's little brother who was only fourteen, wedged into the storage space behind the seats in the jeep and laughed high and girly when his fogged head jounced up and down. But he saw Jenny take Markie's ham-sized hand and place it on her throat, and heard her laugh like jingle bells. So Carl turned his face away and laid his hot cheek against the metal mudguard and looked behind him where the red lights wobbled and the tail pipe hacked and spit, up the long back road to the Tubs.

THE SUMMER WALKED ON, SLOW AND STEADY, KICKING UP A cloud of dust that covered Chester in a thin gritty veil. The leaves of the trees and bushes, which had seemed so bright in June, turned yellow, aghast at the drought. Lawns were balding, brown; and nothing—not car bumpers, not the domed lids of barbecue grills, not the chain-link fence at the elementary school—kept its shine.

Kitten LaPlante ran two fans all day in the house, a giant box fan on the center of the kitchen table, and a smaller round one on the floor of the upstairs hallway. In the last week of July, she lost her job behind the counter at the Home 'N' Farm—an argument with her boss about a pay raise made her cross and she sassed a couple of customers, and then there was a major mistake on a bill—and so the boss, who was also an ex-boyfriend, fired her.

Jenny came home and found Kitten sitting on the living-room couch with a whiskey bottle, pouring the stuff over ice cubes in a tumbler and aggressively gagging it down. She was pretty worked up, talking to herself, with the jazz radio station on full blast. With her long-nailed digits, she stirred the ice in the glass, banging her rings. When she saw Jenny, she told her she'd quit Home 'N' Farm, oh boy, that was enough. She laughed, then burst into tears, moaning she'd been fired by the bastard, just boom like that! The cat hunched under the couch and blinked sullenly at the commotion.

Jenny patted her mother on the shoulder, then got herself some ice and a glass and poured a whiskey to keep her company. But Kitten changed gears. It was as if she had never cried in her life; her voice was clear and filled with rage. She just plain roared, roared at her for drinking, who did she think she was, she was too young, a baby, just trying to make her feel guilty. Like everyone else!

There was obviously no point in hanging around. Jenny grabbed Kitten's handbag and plucked the car keys out, then ran out of the house. The car, an aging boxy sedan, nose-dived down Kenney's Road and then turned west, six miles to South Providence. Marquette and his brother Dan lived over Zax Auto on Route 34, just around the bend from Phelps Corners. The jeep was home, so Jenny pulled in and climbed the steps that led to the second-floor apartment. Dan answered the door.

"He's not here." Dan was older than Markie, a little smaller and better proportioned. But there was something too neat about his hair and ears, something too careful. He was getting a business degree at the community college. Jenny thought he'd be in something low-key, like insurance, and that he'd cheat and steal but would always play it small, and not get caught. She respected him, but he openly disliked her. Now he was eyeing her plaid knickers, her braless tank top, her straw hat, her shades. "You look like a yard sale," he said. He stared at her breasts.

Jenny gave him her smile, and lifted an ankle-strapped foot. "You don't like my new shoes?" she inquired, in a mocking baby voice, turning her ankle for inspection.

"Markie's at the Red Bat with his *friends,*" said Dan. But she knew he was watching her as she swayed down the stairs, ostentatiously careful in her new shoes.

Jenny headed north up 34, then turned up Charley Mountain Road slowly, the car whining in low gear. At the top of Charley Mountain sat a collection of roadside travel stops, including two motels. Just off the road, the old fire-watch tower, its paint fading, carried the sign that read "Charley Summit—Tri-State Views." Below, at the edge of the parking lot, were the stone fences and the big-headed dark green and chrome coin-op binocular machines. The Red Bat, just past the tower on the left, had a churned-up gravel front yard and an ancient flashing red neon sign, of a bat, with wings stretched across the marquee surmounting the front door.

Jenny got stopped by a skinny little guy with bad teeth at the cash register. "I.D.," he said.

Jenny removed her hat and pushed her sunglasses down her nose, and smiled over the rims at him. "Oh, I'm not here to drink. I just want to find my boyfriend," and she pointed to the guys at the pool table.

"Okay, honey." He leaned close and winked. "But don't tell."

His breath was incredible. "Safe as the grave," she said, and winked back. So far everything was fine. It was a great evening. It was smooth, ever since she left the house, smooth as a ball of yarn unwinding, everything she did was linked to everything else, and everyone was going to do exactly what she expected. The humming inside of her head, expectant, distantly tuneful, "Noon by the clock, and so still on the dock . . ."

She walked quietly up to where Markie was about to make his shot. His dark head was lowered in concentration as he sawed the cue stick back and forth across his thumb. While the other guys grinned, she reached down and goosed.

The cue flew up. "Shit, hey, oh shit, you. Shit!"

"Charmed as well, I'm sure."

Krullmeyer laughed so hard his face froze in a grimace and he had to run to the john. Jenny didn't know the other guys, and Markie did not appear to be in an introducing mood. One, in a red plaid shirt, said, "What are you drinking?"

She smiled. "Nothing yet, but a g-and-t would suit me fine."

"Talks like a teacher," muttered a short guy.

"I'm a librarian, actually," said Jenny, and winked broadly at the red plaid shirt as he brought her the drink. She took a long sip.

Markie, who had recovered his dignity with his beer, now spoke: "Don't drink that shit." He took the glass from her. "I'm through here, let's go."

Jenny stood perfectly still and raised her eyebrows at him until he gave her back the drink. She finished it in one gulp, laughed, and said, "Mostly water, anyway." Then, turning to the shirt, asked, "What do I owe you?" He seemed confused. Jenny pulled two dollars from her wallet, waved them: "Will this cover it?"

He finally spoke: "Oh no—no, no. I've got it. No." He blushed.

That's right, thought Jenny as she grabbed Markie's hand and pretended that he was dragging her out of the bar. It was on the house. Complimentary. The entire evening is complimentary. Except, for the moment, Markie.

"Fucking show-off," he snorted as he opened the driver's door.

"It's my mother's car, and I'll drive it!"

"Fucking bossy show-off bitch." But he walked around to the other side. On the ride down the mountain Jenny told him, with a throb in her voice, about Kitten losing her job. That cooled Markie down immediately and he began saying things like Hey, too bad, and patting her hand on the steering wheel.

III PIRATE JENNY III

They pulled into the lot in front of Zax. The jeep was gone. Markie shifted awkwardly in his seat. "Come up for a beer?" It was such a tiny question.

An hour later, in the half-light, Markie breathing so heavily he sounded asthmatic, Jenny's back gridded with ridges from his bedspread, both of them down to their underpants, Jenny well over the giggles, gasping for breath, her teeth and gums rubbed so hard by Markie's tongue it felt like the dentist—she spoke:

"Maybe I should get a prescription for the pill."

Markie held his hands at her waist. It took him a minute. "Uh. Oh. I got some rubbers." He almost fell off the bed, then lurched towards the dresser.

This is it, she thought. Oh. No. The sudden absence of Markie from her side was like getting off a boat and still feeling the waves. For the first time, she felt real desire, indistinguishable from pain. She stood, and staggered to the dresser, where Markie was carefully fitting the condom. "What is my name?" she demanded. "Jenny Jenny Jenny," he said, as he pushed her back on the bed and fell heavily on top of her.

When Dan came home an hour later, he stamped noisily on the wooden steps. He opened the door and saw Jenny, fully dressed, sitting at the kitchen table and smoking a joint, leafing through his new skin magazine.

"Have some?" Jenny offered Dan the joint but he frowned no and opened the fridge for a beer. After a while Markie came sleepily into the kitchen, looking confused.

"Hey, any left?" He poked in the ashtray for the butt, pulled it out, and bit it precariously between his teeth while he tried to light it.

Jenny turned to Dan. "Can we borrow your jeep?"

"Let *him* ask me."

"Shit, Dan, can we take the jeep?" Dan said nothing, just unbuttoned his front shirt pocket, took out the keys, and threw them on the table. He went into his bedroom and shut the door. They heard the TV come on.

"Where did you want to go?"

"Just out."

They drove to the river and found a place to park. They stared at the water as it moved slowly around in its enormous dry bed.

"Looks like black today," Markie finally said.

"No, it's purple, actually. It looks darker because the light's going. I saw it earlier. Royal purple."

Markie cleared his throat uncomfortably, and they stared at the water. He put his hand on Jenny's shoulder, but she pulled away.

"Markie, what am I going to do?"

"About your mother? I don't think there's much . . ."

"No. About me. I can't take much more of this. I feel so trapped."

"Well, shit, if you're talking about . . . well, you don't have to feel trapped. I'm the one that's supposed to feel trapped."

"No, no. You never understand. Not you. That wasn't it. It's everything else."

"Sure I understand. But senior year—it'll be great, you know. It's the best. And then I'll come home for—leave—you know."

Jenny's impulse to confide subsided. What had she imagined—that the long interval of grunting and gasping which had just transpired, the shocking, painful, good news she had learned, that this was going to carry along, like that single strand of yarn, into everything else? How could she

III PIRATE JENNY III

tell him about what she needed to have, to be? An image from a catalogue, of a marble bathtub with brass fixtures, orchids in a vase on lace, a smell of perfume, crowded with the idea of floating effortlessly through. . . .

But Markie interrupted. "You could join the Navy too, maybe, next year?"

"See the world."

"Sure. We'll get on the same ship, and nobody'll know about us, right? And we'll sail to Shanghai and Madrid and Greece . . ."

"Greece!"

"We'll go ashore and have a white stone house on the beach and drink wine."

"And you'll fight duels for me with shipping tycoons! And you'll be wounded, with a scar. Or no—I'll fight them, too, two musketeers, but I won't get a scar."

"I think you're really really pretty."

Jenny fell silent, then rummaged in the glove compartment for a joint. She punched in the lighter and waited for it to pop, then lit the joint and inhaled deeply. She held the glowing lighter up to Markie's face, which got very pink then faded into shadow as the lighter cooled.

"You're not looking bad yourself, you know, Marquette?" She snorted. "See the world."

They puffed on the joint, while the crickets and the river chirped and hushed, like a big wave buoying the jeep somewhere else. Then the mosquitoes got bad, and they drove back.

Much later, Jenny stared at the ceiling of her room. She kicked around in the heat, and pushed the sheet off the bed. Downstairs, Kitten, who had wakened with an early hangover, was brewing coffee and making muffled, demanding phone calls—to old boyfriends, to the Dads, to her mother, to girlfriends. But no one wanted to talk at that late hour, and so Kitten kept slamming the phone back into the cradle—then, worried that she had disturbed her daughter, she would look anxiously up the stairs at her bedroom door.

3

THEY WERE AT THE TUBS ON A SUNDAY
afternoon. The main waterfall had subsided to its midsummer trickle, and the aspens and birches were statue-still against the cobalt sky. At least it looked cobalt through Jenny's sunglasses, and the styro cooler looked fuchsia. Cobalt, she said to herself, and again remembered the day last winter when she and Kitten had driven all the way to Boston so Kitten could see an old high school friend, Gail Bouchard, only now it was Gail Hinzmann. She took them to tea at the Ritz—Jenny guessed that it *used* to be in Paris, when they made all the old movies, but now it had moved to Boston.

The water glasses were cobalt blue—"Lovely cobalt

blue," said Kitten shyly, stroking a stem, not wanting to move her head around and gape. Jenny was thrilled but terrified, and knew that her winter boots were puddling on the carpet. The other women, including Gail, were wearing delicate little shoes, Gail's were even suede—how did they maneuver through the slush?—but she and Kitten wore their boots, Kitten's with tassels on the zippers. Those burgundy vinyl boots with two-inch stacked heels and tattered tassels looked incredibly ugly on the fawn-colored carpet. Jenny had never seen anything so ugly, except maybe her own boots, black rubber with creamy fleece lining at the top, new, but like a battleship is new. Gunboats, she thought, remembering a song the Dads used to sing— "Your feet's too big."

Gail was perfectly groomed, smooth, with smooth red hair that was tied back from her face with a silky scarf, and big golden triangles on her ears and a necklace of big golden circles around her neck. She pointed at creamy cakes and fruit tarts, and the waiter used silver tongs to transfer them from the silver cart with wheels. She poured the tea for them all, from a white china pot ringed with a stripe of the same rich blue and another stripe of gold. Gail's nails were pretty, smooth, and after she poured the tea she held her arms perfectly still along the arms of her chair, the hands just hanging there like empty gloves off the ends.

Kitten drank sherry instead of tea, and her nose got pink as she laughed with Gail about high school. Jenny knew that her mother had been the prettiest girl in high school—she had seen the yearbook, heard all the stories—but she knew that what Gail had now was better than pretty, it was like a magazine makeover on her whole life, it was beautiful. Jenny stared at the silverware—she checked, and it said "sterling" on the back—and drank from her heavy cobalt water glass, the lip as thick as her own. When she got up enough courage, she looked around, and saw dozens of beautiful women with beautiful dresses and hands and hair, murmuring at the tables around the room. On the walls hung great heroic paintings: battle scenes; ships at sea; a stern double portrait of an elderly couple; a bewigged crowd of men, a herd of George Washingtons, standing around and looking pleased with themselves, regarding a document held by the man in the middle. The chandeliers were fitted with white Christmas-tree bulbs, and among the clear white crystal tears a few cobalt drops also fell.

While the women talked, Jenny turned her chair towards the tall French windows that faced a park. Beneath huge trees, white snowy ground was being misted with rain. She watched the fur coats go by, some carrying parcels, some pushing strollers, some getting into taxis. Jenny relaxed enough to sigh, wiggle back in her chair, and say to herself, pompously: I could be very comfortable here.

But then it was time to leave. She panicked, briefly, about what piece of silverware she would steal, before settling on a dessert fork because it had an asymmetrical hump on one side that made it look classy. She tucked it into the fleece of her boot, and it scraped her calf through her tights as she followed Gail and Kitten to the cloakroom.

She scratched her calf in the same place, and made the sunburn redder. Markie was lying on his back.

"You've got a spare tire and it's falling out of your trunk!" Jenny pinched the soft brown fold.

"No sir," said Markie, as he sucked in his breath and stood up, inflating his chest. "No flab here." Jenny slid down the slick chute to the next pool, a skinny otter over pink sandstone, and laughed heartlessly.

After that, Markie went to the library and found a military exercise manual from the Korean War. When he got up in the morning, and again in midafternoon, he ran through a series of sit-ups, push-ups, arm rolls, and deep knee bends. At the toy store in the mall, he bought a candy-striped skip rope. Frowning, holding his breath, he counted fifty red-hot peppers while the bells in the handles tinkled.

AUGUST WAS A BLANKET OF RAIN. THE RIVER SWELLED FOR A week of heavy rain, and then a flash downpour flooded the paper mill. Chester residents climbed up Beech Hill above the highway to take pictures of the long low brick building with its many-paned windows sunk halfway into the dark brown swirl. The road's own snaky curves were for three days obliterated by water, and the business of clearing away the trees and rocks took more than a week. One person died in the flood, an old black woman named Mrs. Scarborough, who had lived for years in a tar-paper shack halfway up the Blue to the Tubs. The house got stuck in the weir below the mill, but Mrs. Scarborough and her three goats washed up in the woods several miles down, by Sander's meadows. They were found in a group by Charlie Sander's Labrador, Sugar, who ate part of a goat and got violently sick before running home to tell Charlie.

Pretty soon the excitement over the flood died down, but no one could get over how the sky stayed grey. Kitten was furious, because she had promised herself the month as a sort of vacation while she collected on unemployment, talking vaguely about camping and swimming. Instead she was stuck in the house, drinking, for two straight weeks of rain. She gave up her vacation and began to look for another job. There was part-time work as a nurse's aide at the Sweetwater Nursing Home in South Providence, with lousy pay and the bad night shifts, but she took it, claiming there were possibilities for advancement.

Her late hours gave Jenny more time alone. She couldn't seem to read anymore, not even her closet stash of novels, but took to playing her music very loud, singing and dancing until two or three in the morning. She never invited Markie over to the house, and this summer she had allowed her other friendships to lapse. But she was not alone. Recently she had filched from the library a big coffee-table book about Berlin in the 1920s and 1930s, which contained a photograph of Lotte Lenya and Kurt Weill just prior to their emigration to the United States. Jenny knew about World War II, and of course about Hitler, though his name indicated something other than a man. "Hitler"—as in "They fled Hitler," or "Before Hitler"—took on the quality of a natural disaster, like a hurricane or a flood; or it was just a convenient temporal marker, like "the turn of the century." It just seemed to Jenny—as she turned the pages and stared at the assembled artists and intellectuals and actors and who-knew-whats sitting at cafés, smirking and puffing on cigarettes and drinking, or lounging on couches in dim salons, or rushing with hands shoved into their pockets down narrow, glamorous streets—a shame that Weill and Lenya had been forced to leave such a glamorous, wicked world.

Mahagonny was set in an imaginary America; Jenny felt entitled to concoct scraps of stories set in an imaginary Germany. She cut the portrait from the book, found it a plastic box frame, and hung it over her bed one sticky August night. The bespectacled Weill had a kind of mild, inquisitive look; Lenya, with her face turned aside, her lips dark red and pressed together, her arms crossed, looked like a wild thing barely able to hold herself back from flight. Jenny fiddled with her hair for a long time to see if she could approximate the marcelled bangs that rolled above Lenya's painted brows, snipping bits off with her nail scissors until she looked like an alarmed friar.

Markie drove all the way to Lincoln for his second physical ("just a formality," he boasted), passed, and was told to report to the base in Delaware on September 20. Meanwhile, Kitten's new boyfriend, Mel Suzewski (brother of the truck driver), got her a VCR. Mel managed the J&S Audio in the shopping center in Charleytown. He also told her she could have a job there just as soon as the clerk who was pregnant quit to have her baby. Kitten spent days agonizing about whether she should, again, work for someone she was dating. The dilemma was compounded by the presence of the son of a Sweetwater patient, a lawyer from Lincoln, who seemed interested. And everyone said how good she looked in the aide's uniform, how the white coat set off her dark eyes and hair and her trim figure.

Jenny had long since learned not to say too much to Kitten in the way of advice, and she listened to the radio while her mother talked. Jenny personally was in favor of J&S Audio; the VCR thrilled her. Jenny granted Markie dispensation and let him in the house to watch movies, which he rented for them. Jenny discovered Marlene Dietrich in *Lili Marlene* and *The Blue Angel* and *Desire* and was riveted to learn that she spoke the way she sang, that German lilt— mocking, sexy. She guttered her g's and w's, like Lenya, but she also had an Elmer Fudd lisp on her r's. After Markie left one night, Jenny stayed up and replayed sections of *Rancho Notorious.* Marlene kissed the cowboy: "That's for trying." Then she slapped him, viciously: "That's for trying too

||| PIRATE JENNY |||

hard." "Haaawd," whispered Jenny in the blue light, mush-
ing the r. "Tu haaawd."

During her last week of work at the Root Beer Barn,
Jenny overheard George making plans to visit New York
City over the Labor Day weekend, with his buddy Mike.
That Saturday, the last Saturday of August, George closed
the Barn at five and hosted an end-of-summer party for the
girls. He and Mike and Val's brother drove everybody in a
van and a pickup and a car down to Lake Moosic. It was a
chilly day, really autumnal, so no one brought a swimsuit
but three of the girls brought boys. Jenny had not asked
Markie. She managed to nab the front seat of the van and
talked nicely to Mike as he drove, asking questions about
what George had been like in "school," which she knew to
mean college. George had been a history major; he had
played on the baseball team; he had had two steady girlfriends in four years. She was pleased that Mike was selling
his friend to her; he thought she was sweet on him.

The public docks on Moosic were under a stand of very
tall pines on the end of the lake that narrowed, like a neck,
to the river that flowed from it. The docks were pretty
dilapidated; there were no other big boats, only a couple of
rowboats for fishing. Jenny felt the pine needles bounce
under her feet as she hopped from the van, eyeing
George's little cabin cruiser dubiously. It was chipped-
paint white, with a high platform on top—for deep-sea
fishing, Mike explained, and all the guys cracked up. The
boat's name, *Annabel Lee,* was painted on the side.

Jenny smiled at George. "Is this the kingdom by the
sea?"

He looked startled. What a jerk, Jenny thought. "Sure,"
he said. "Why not?" He looked at her head. "Where's the

ponytail, kiddo?" He ran his hand along her short bangs, and then pulled back, embarrassed. Jenny thought if he blushed any deeper he'd pass out.

Once on his boat, George was filled with a kind of alien energy, tying and untying ropes (though they never left the dock), mixing drinks, fiddling with the engine, and cutting up with Mike and the other guys—Deboise and two guys from Lincoln who were visiting Val and Val's brother. They pushed Val's brother into the lake and sang and ignored the girls until much later, when everyone was drunk and the radio box they'd set on the dock was tuned to a love-songs station. Everybody clutched and danced. Then the extra girls stripped to their undies and went swimming, squealing about the cold and the muck on the bottom of the lake. So of course the guys stopped dancing and joined *them.* Except for George, captain of the ship, who stayed on board the whole time. And Jenny.

Jenny slid an arm around George's waist. "Can I ask you a question? It's sort of personal." George looked solicitous. "You see, my mother—" Jenny gulped, and said quickly, "It's, she's got a new boyfriend, you know, and he's there tonight, and they—like—make lots of noise and stuff, so I was wondering could I stay with you?"

"Um." George burped, softly. "I was gonna stay on my boat tonight."

Jenny smiled as if that answered it, and said, "Okay by me."

When they were all alone—after the smirking and the wisecracks as everyone piled into the van and the car, including, reluctantly, Sandy, who'd had the biggest crush on George all summer and who lamely suggested that they could *all* stay on the boat tonight—the lake was quiet with mist, and there were no stars for gazing. George began to

III P I R A T E   J E N N Y III

bustle importantly, putting a pillow on the bunk below for Jenny, spreading a blanket out on the deck for himself. Feeling something ice-cold inside her, Jenny choreographed her movements a split-second ahead of time: Kneel beside George on the blanket, pull his mouth onto mine, collapse backward with him. She closed her eyes so she couldn't see his pale lashes in the light of the kerosene lantern, his wide blondness. She imagined instead that he was Gary Cooper in *Morocco,* imagined like mad—and eventually, mercifully, her body took over and she didn't have to think at all.

Waking cold and wet with George and a hangover gave Jenny a new definition of a bad time. They dressed and spruced, as well as they could, and drove to a place for coffee. George did not stop apologizing.

"You know, it's policy—I don't date the girls. I *never* did that. It was—I was drunk. You came on kinda strong. I'm sorry. We were both drunk, kiddo. I know it was unfair of me. I'm sorry. You're just a kid. Oh, God, I'm sorry, kiddo."

On her second cup of coffee, Jenny said, "Can I go with you to New York?"

George looked puzzled for a minute, then his face cleared. "Oh, New *York.* That's a trip me and Mike are—well, gee, no. Actually, it's just a guys' trip, thing."

"I really want to go."

"Jenny, I'm sorry, but no. Anyway, listen—" He pulled himself upright in his chair and looked stern. "That's really no place for a young girl. Plus, you know, they dress very very sharp there, you know?"

"What's the matter with how I dress?" Her tone was much too snappish.

"Nothing, sure. But you should see the women on, like,

Madison Avenue. I mean, they dress like *models.* Some of them *are* models!"

It was the hangover and the disappointment. Jenny lost control. "There was this fashion consultant on a talk show? And he listed the ten biggest fashion errors, and for your information, *sir,* I don't make one. Not one. And I'm the individualistic type, which as everyone knows all through the ages has been the most stylish no matter what the style was."

George looked at her pityingly, and he laughed. "A talk show!"

Nuts, she thought, remembering too late an adage from the Dads: Never reveal your sources. Nuts. Jenny sulked all the way back to Chester. As she watched the same drab banks of dirt and trees that edged the road go by, in the fog that lifted as the morning wore along, she thought about her father, silently blaming him. It really was his fault. She thought about how everyone said he was "good with people," which meant he always sort of impressed them. How she had watched, at a little distance, in the old days when he lived at home, and friends would come over and laugh. All of his men friends told stories over their beer. Johnny would tell how he'd been to the circus in Lincoln, how there were twenty elephants and they held on to one another's tails and marched in a line, pulling the tiger cages. And she couldn't stay quiet, but would squeal, "Dads, Dads, can we go to the circus?" and he'd pull her on his lap, and start to tell his own story. How he, Frank, had an aunt who used to work in the circus, high-wire act, and how he'd gotten a job with her once. He'd been a clown; did Johnny know that all the elephants were on tranquilizers? That the tigers took Quaaludes and when they got restless late at night, when the drugs wore off, only Frank and one other guy were brave enough to feed them their raw steaks and calm them down.

Sure, thought Jenny bitterly, he's good with people, only no one ever believed a thing he said and he doesn't have any money. When they got to Kenney's Road, she made George drive her all the way up, even though his pickup almost wept in low gear.

Explaining the night on the boat to Markie was easy. "I'd had too much to drink," she said, "and I got sick in the lake. So I lay down on the bunk and while I was asleep everyone left. But George slept on the deck. You know I wouldn't let him touch me," and here she giggled confidingly. "He has blond eyelashes." Markie was proud of his own dark lashes, like the glue-on ones sold in drugstores. "Plus," said Jenny, giggling harder, "he was too drunk to move."

On Monday she went to the Root Beer Barn to get her things, and made one last try. She had a hard time assuming her usual banter with George, because she found him physically disgusting now; his red-haired arms almost made her gag. She shouldn't have bothered. Dismissively, in his best college-boy style, he told her again that he would not take her along to New York and left the office, letting the door slam shut behind him as he went about his important business.

Jenny was furious. She thought for a moment. She turned the volume up on the radio, and began gently going through the drawers of the office desk. The petty-cash box was in the bottom left. She had the grey metal lid up and saw a couple of fifties and some tens. She reached.

George opened the door. Jenny jumped a foot and slammed the drawer.

"Oh please," he said. "Not really. Looking for something?"

"No."

"Money? Were you looking for money?"

Jenny's mind blanked. "Actually, yes," she said. "Actually, I need money"—she looked straight into George's eyes—"for an abortion."

He blinked. "You do not. Go to a clinic. You're lying. You're so full of bullshit."

Jenny avoided his eyes and fled. Later in the week the talk got back to her: George and Mike and *Sandy* had all gone down to the Big Apple for the Big Weekend.

JENNY BEGAN HER SENIOR YEAR OF HIGH SCHOOL THE TUESDAY after Labor Day. The bus picked her up along with two other kids at the bottom of Kenney's Road and carted them a few miles east to the regional high school, whose students came from Chester, Sagatuck, Charleytown, and Sayville. Everything was exactly familiar: the long fluorescent corridors, the dull yellow walls, the thick elastic on the gym shorts, the smell.

Bradley Dill, the shop instructor, elbowed history teacher Irene Peche in the stomach when he sighted Jenny coming down the corridor, fresh from an introduction to lacrosse. Jenny's hair, still wet from the shower, was slicked down in stringy ringlets where she had tried to mousse it, and she had wrapped an old silk necktie around her head. Her pale eyes stared straight ahead with military blankness. Her short nails were polished black, and her plaid knickers ended just above her tall black vinyl boots with spike heels, the ones Markie had ordered from a catalogue. The boots didn't fit and she swaggered uncertainly. Her mouth was outlined in black, the contours filled in with bright red lipstick.

||| PIRATE JENNY |||

"Jesus fucking Christ on a crutch," observed Dill.

"Is that the new look? It couldn't be," said Peche. "No. Nobody else looks remotely like that this year." She tittered and sent a shiny-eyed glance at Dill. "She must have made that one up, all by herself."

Before the end of that first terrible day, Jenny knocked the heels off the boots against the cement wall behind the cafeteria. At least then she could walk straight.

The last night before Markie left, the crowd gathered at the dump for a send-off. Debbie D. brought sparklers and a tiny American flag. Krullmeyer, Deboise, Crutcher, Jimmy Johnson, and Eddie Feehan sang:

> *"Anchors aweigh, my boy,*
> *Anchors aweigh.*
> *If you get stuck inside your port of call,*
> *Just grab your dick and haul haul haul.*
> *You're a first class seaman now, my boy,*
> *So anchors aweigh!"*

Then they showered him with a confetti of tinfoil condom packets. Val presented the real gift: three ounces of California mushrooms, enclosed in an old hollowed-out hardback copy of *Cathy Miller, Navy Nurse*.

Markie gave everyone a chip of mushroom, and they all got silly—the girls dancing to the car radio and the guys shouting boasts and climbing up the little peaked roof of Eddie's shack. Crutcher danced close with Jenny, and began breathing fast. He slobbered on her ear, and she laughed.

Eventually Markie and Jenny drove home to Jenny's house. She poured them some of Kitten's whiskey and they screwed on the rag rug in the living room, dizzily, awkwardly, elbowing one another. Markie cut his knee on the driftwood coffee table getting up. Jenny slapped the cat away from the mushrooms and took another bite. She lay nude on the rug.

"The only thing that departed from good taste in the evening's festivities was—that spot on Corey's midriff," she remarked. Markie wandered in from the kitchen, swigging from a liter bottle of diet cola. "Did she know it was there?" she continued. "If so, why reveal it? Was it a rash? A hickey? The mark of Cain?" She laughed and laughed and rolled onto her side, laughing.

"Sorry about the guys," said Markie, as he sat down on the couch, which was strewn with condom packets. "That's just old-fashioned guy shit, you know, girl in every port. You don't have to worry."

Jenny sat up and pulled on her T-shirt. "Oh, Markie, I don't worry about you. I don't—vurrrry—at all." She liked it better without the lisp.

4

A BETTER IDEA CAME TO JENNY AS SHE sat in assembly, in the school's beige-curtained and blue-seated auditorium. The new superintendent was gesticulating about school spirit to a stony-faced crowd, occasionally raising his fist in the gesture that had earned him the nickname "Mighty Mouse." The Mouse wore a striped blue-and-white shirt—he had removed his jacket the better to exhort—and Jenny was hypnotized by the lines. It was something in the notion of "parallel," a remembered thrill from geometry class last year, that a line could run side by side with another forever and they'd never meet. She began to imagine a line running along the stage, while another ran behind the beige asbestos curtain. She imagined lines on a map, a route following a line of longitude.

Something popped open, like the shutter on a door to a nightclub or a fortress, and Jenny looked through to the life inside. She began to make out a figure that was hers, doing things with swiftness and confidence, as in a movie. She couldn't tell exactly what it was, but piece by piece the focus sharpened and she saw an envelope, a marble staircase, a car. Later, on the lacrosse field, Jenny turned suddenly—it was as if she had heard music piping to her from over the Patty Mountains. She shook her head like a cow shakes off flies, listening. She stared up and away, shaking her head, muttering, eyes shining, while the gym teacher and her entire team screamed her name.

It was odd, she discovered over the next few days. She could best go into the trance, to think and plan, when there were other people around. She enjoyed floating away from a needy world, but she learned to compose her features into an unremarkable blank when it happened. And so she planned it, step by step.

Meanwhile, Kitten stayed with the nursing-home job, after all. It was full day shifts now, but the lawyer's mother died, and her big-shot son in the good suits vanished. Jenny listened while Kitten complained, and astonished her mother by confiding in her about school and girlfriends. When Markie's first postcard came, she read it aloud.

> Dear Jenny, This is the barracks where we sleep and drill and eat. Pretty exciting, right? The arrow shows me, lying on my bunk and dreaming of you. My friend Paul and all the guys here want to see pictures, so send some if you can. See you soon I hope, Thanksgiving. Best, Markie.

III PIRATE JENNY III

On the morning of October 1, a Wednesday, Jenny woke up very early, before her alarm. She looked automatically at the clock, which read ten to five. She had lain stiff as a board all night on her stomach, and both her arms had gone to sleep. She thrashed around under the covers to loosen the dead weights, then sat up and shook her limbs. She reached over to turn off the alarm button, while her arms stung and shook inside.

In a minute she was dressed in T-shirt, jeans, sweater, gloves, and sneakers. Her bag, mostly empty, was ready, and she picked it up and walked very softly down the stairs. Kitten's handbag was on the coffee table in the living room. Jenny unzipped it and extracted the car keys, feeling clumsy in the stiff gloves. Then she went into the kitchen, dampened a paper towel at the sink, and wiped the sleepy seed out of her eyes. She poured a glass of grapefruit juice, downed it, and then gently opened the front door, gently pulled it shut behind her, and gently padded down the steps.

It was one of those fall mornings when a mist lies over everything, and sounds carry. The latch on the car door seemed ridiculously loud. Jenny got in, put her bag on the seat beside her, but didn't close the door. Kitten always parked in reverse, the head of the car pointed down the driveway. Jenny turned the key partway, pushed in the clutch, and set the car in neutral. It started to roll, slowly, out the drive and down Kenney's Road. Jenny stood on the brake until just past the Tarleton house. Then she turned the car off the road, pointing upwards in the roll above the ditch, slammed the door, and started the engine.

Down on Route 9, the fog floated over the river and the road like white scarves. There were no other cars all the way to South Providence. Just before the Route 34 intersection, down by the river, sat an abandoned shed that had once been a produce stand. Jenny pulled the car in behind the shed, into the vines and scrub oaks. It was virtually invisible from the road.

With Markie's door key in one hand and her suitcase in the other, Jenny walked along the gravel shoulder of the highway about fifty yards, until she could see the Zax sign around a clump of trees on the other side of the road. As she put a foot on the pavement, she heard the distant sound of a car. She turned, almost fell down the embankment, and lay down in the bushes. What passed by was an old grey sedan, the one that Mrs. Delray used for her taxi service. It dragged by, tail pipe almost hitting the ground. Jenny was sure that the passenger in the backseat turned his head to look in her direction. Her heart almost stopped, as she tried to formulate the words that she would say: I'm just picking flowers. No. What?

But the car was gone. She allowed herself to sigh, then started to reach for the suitcase that had fallen from her hand, when another sound made her fall flat again. A truck, not from the mill but sleek white and green, a gasoline truck, thundered by, well over the forty-five speed limit.

Then the hush was absolute again. Not waiting for another surprise, Jenny grabbed her case and ran across the road to Zax. She placed the case onto the front seat of the jeep. Quickly, silently, she climbed the steps and let herself in.

The kitchen clock said five-twenty. Jenny rummaged around carefully on the table and counter but couldn't find the keys. Dan's shirt was on the floor under one of the kitchen chairs. Yes; the keys were in the pocket, one ring of car keys, one of house keys. She smiled. Then she opened the refrigerator door and flipped up the lid on the butter

III P I R A T E J E N N Y III

compartment. There it was: the envelope with Dan's cash. She did not wait to count it, but held it in her hand with the keys and slinked back out. She stuck Dan's house keys into the lock on the door, so it looked as if he had forgotten them there.

The jeep roared when she started it and gunned it with gas to get it into gear. She swung back out onto Route 9 and headed east, back through Chester, east past the library, the SuperSave, Kenney's Road, the mill, the Root Beer Barn, the shopping strip, the high school. She pulled into the parking lot at the Sayville post office and sealed up the keys to Kitten's car in an envelope with the note she had written last night:

> Dear Mom,
> Here's the car keys. It's behind the old farmstand on 9. I'm sorry but I had to leave. I'll be okay, so don't worry. You know I can take care of myself.
> Love,
> Connie
> P.S. Don't let the Dads be such a leech. He's a liar and a jerk.

It would take at least two days to get to the LaPlante mailbox less than ten miles away. She counted Dan's money: $280, with a bonus of two joints in the envelope. At the turnoff in Sayville, she took a right and headed south on the connector to the interstate. It was six A.M. She headed southwest for a long way.

Somewhere in Connecticut, Jenny pulled in at a mall, a huge, sprawling brick fortification. She parked the jeep and got out, wandering in through one of the glass doors that parted automatically before her, like water. In the midst of a dizzying concatenation of escalators, elevators, and stairs, and skylights and tall wan trees and Formica-tiled fountains, she found a directory and went off in search of a hair salon.

A young woman reading a newspaper sat behind the counter at The Hair Force.

"A—cut and dye job, please," Jenny announced.

"Got an appointment?"

"No."

"Ten minutes. Take a seat," she said, pointing to the brown-and-chrome chairs. Jenny perched on the edge of a chair with her handbag in her lap. There were only two other customers in the salon, both older women. Jenny fingered one of the yellow mums that banked the plate-glass window. It was some kind of cloth. She picked up a fashion magazine and stared at it.

"Miss? Miss? Rufus is ready." Rufus, a young man who looked Korean, was wearing a dark brown lab smock. He snapped his long steel scissors in Jenny's direction and gestured her into a chair. An underling taped up Jenny's neck like a priest's and dropped a light brown tent over her body. Rufus circled her, picking up the ends of her hair and dropping them with distaste. "Who cut your hair last?"

She did not answer but pulled the magazine out from under her tent and pointed to a photo of a very tall model in a kilt walking seven Irish setters. She was tilted backwards and grinning wildly. "I want one like that," said Jenny. "Only with short curled bangs. Dyed dark red."

"Not *dark* red," admonished Rufus.

"Yes. Like blood, dark red."

He sighed. "Whatever. Wash it!" The minion returned, shuffling, and led Jenny to a sink in the back. The attendant was an older woman who breathed heavily as she pushed

Jenny under the hose. Jenny's hair was swamped under several tides of shampoo and rinse and conditioner that smelled strongly of almonds. Then her hair was squeezed and wrapped in a dark brown towel and she was led back to Rufus.

"Here we go." He snipped apparently aimlessly, sometimes lunging in with a sharp exhale, like a fencer. Jenny frowned. Eventually a twenties bob appeared, decorated with a short fringe on top. Rufus blow-dried, then handed the dryer to the attendant while he stood off to one side and mixed the color.

"Not highlights? All-over color?"

"All over."

With a paintbrush stirring goo that looked like barbecue sauce, Rufus returned and began painting and pinning Jenny's hair. "This is not a contemporary look. This will be a classical look." Jenny did not reply.

An hour later, after her plastic-capped head had baked under a heat lamp, Jenny's hair was brushed out, moussed, sprayed, brushed out, shaped, and sprayed. It looked like an enormous red mushroom cap. Jenny frowned. "I want it down, close to my head." Rufus wet it, brushed it down, gelled it, dried it, gelled it, and brushed it down. "Better?"

"Yes, fine," said Jenny.

"It looks like you slept on it," said Rufus, turning away in disgust. Jenny went to the front desk and paid the $55 for cut and color. Then she walked to the hair washer and handed her a dollar. "Thank you very much," she said.

There were several clothing boutiques from which to choose. Jenny went into one called The Lady Eve, and found exactly what she needed in the Career & Campus sale rack. She selected a white blouse with a round collar, and a full charcoal-grey circle skirt and a navy pleated skirt, both of which stopped just above the ankles. A pair of taupe panty hose, an underwire bra, white, and some white underpants. A pair of grey knee-socks, cable-stitched. Then a slate-blue cardigan sweater. The whole thing came to $120. Jenny handed over the cash. Then with her big shopping bag full of clothes, she dawdled in the store until the salesgirl's back was turned. She slipped four more blouses, two more pairs of hose, some knee socks, and two extra cardigans—one yellow, one grey—into the bag.

The glass door jingled a bell when she opened it. "Goodbye now," Jenny called to the salesgirl, and smiled.

On another level, Jenny found a store called The Shoe Box. A pair of low black pumps was $80. Holding the shoes aloft contemplatively, she looked quickly to see if she was being watched. Wait for the woman buying the slippers to go to the register. Now. She switched the gummed stickers on the sole with the sticker from a pair of slingbacks, $35, and bought the pumps. She found Gentleman's Gentleman and bought a small-brimmed gray fedora with a thin black ribbon at the band.

"Cross-dressing?" inquired the clerk, with a leer. Jenny stared at him blankly. The hat was $32. Jenny handed him two twenties. As he gave her the change, she threw him the smile.

"I'm so sorry," she said, beaming. "I gave you three twenties. I need the change. Can you give me fives?" This was pushing it. It wouldn't work. But the clerk stared confusedly into the till, then counted out five extra fives. "That's one too many," she giggled, and handed him back a bill. "You wouldn't want me to *cheat* you?"

He smiled back dumbly and shook his head. "I'm just crazy about red hair," he said. Jenny left the store, waving. In a pharmacy, she shoplifted some new makeup and a couple of candy bars and paid ninety cents for a newspaper and a pack of gum.

It was around noon. Jenny went into a restaurant that was fixed up with yellow cracked-glass gas lamps and heavy oak booths, The Lion and the Lamb. A waiter wearing a striped shirt with sleeve garters brought her the Pub Lunch Menu. Jenny counted her money, discovering that only $50 of Dan's was left. She had only another $50 of her own. Bangers and mash with soup and salad cost $6.50. Jenny picked at the gravy-laden potatoes and reviewed her situation.

She was obsessed with the term "paper trail." Surely she had done everything in her power this past week, but she went over it again. Every snapshot of her in the photo album and the loose, disorganized drawer of pictures Kitten hadn't bothered with since Frank left—Jenny had burned them in the hibachi. Likewise the school papers, report cards, childhood drawings. It probably wasn't necessary, but it felt exhilarating to see the past disappear. And she had cleaned, God she had cleaned, washed every dish in the house, spray-dusted every surface, trying to think like a detective—everything she had ever touched, wiped clean. In those awful rubber gloves. It had been a mistake to try to burn them, too—she had had to bury the melted remains up on the hill. But surely nobody would care enough to look there. Her library card, her school I.D., her bank book, driver's licence, her social security card. She had burned or melted and buried them all.

Kitten had been amazed at her cleaning energy, though of course she missed the funeral pyres. Late last night, after she had already packed and lain down, Jenny remembered the car. She had sneaked down with a wet rag and mopped everywhere, cursing the sticky fake leather seats. And then she had wiped down the outside of the car, leaving the driver's door open so she could get a little light, feeling like an idiot. She washed her hands at the kitchen sink, lathering them over and over, and wondering what she had forgotten when she was remembering fingerprints. She went into the shoe box in the closet under the stairs and got out Kitten's new gloves, thin pigskin, a present from the Dads last Christmas that Kitten never wore because they were too nice to ruin. They fit Jenny fine.

Fatigue catching up with her, she asked for coffee and took her parcels into the rest room. She changed into a blouse and the grey skirt and the blue cardigan. The shoes were too tight over the knee socks, so she put on the hose. Then she jammed the hat down over the hair, level, and snapped the front brim up in a crescent. She lined her eyes, mascaraed her lashes, and lipsticked her mouth dark red.

"Vunderbar," she said. "Fucking vunderbar." She stuffed her other clothes in the shopping bag—wiping every button on the sweater with her gloved fingers. Unrecognizable, she left the restaurant.

In the parking lot, she extracted her T-shirt from the shopping bag, spit on it, and damp-mopped the shiny blue surfaces of the jeep. How long did fingerprints last? Would rain wash them away? Was rain predicted? Was there a thumb mark from last summer when Markie had kissed her the first time and she had banged her knee on the steering wheel?

She pulled her small bag out from the back of the jeep and opened it. She had packed only her Weill-Lenya tapes and her cassette player and their framed photo. There was just enough room for all the new clothes. She stopped dead. Something she had not thought of. What to do? Ah. Okay. She stuck the key back into the ignition of the jeep and left it there, a present to the mall. With any luck, some-body would take it.

Her arms had begun to shake and she had to stop and breathe deeply, leaning against the door. She crumpled the shopping bag around her old clothes and stuffed them into a trash bin. Then she picked up her suitcase and walked away.

At the other end of the interstate exit from the mall was a truck stop. The drivers from a line of semis out front were parked on stools at the counter when Jenny walked in. In a little-girl voice, she asked the cashier, a large woman, "Could someone give me a ride to New York? I lost my bus money."

"Anyone heading to New York?" yelled the cashier. Several men swiveled to look at Jenny and sniggered. Then a man stood up from a booth, saying, "Sure, I'm going to the city." Jenny saw that he wore good black loafers, khakis, a pink dress shirt without a tie, and a gold wristwatch on a leather strap. He was darkly tanned with short dark hair. She couldn't take it all in, however, because her attention went immediately to his mouth. The muscles around his lips were pinched broadly back, giving his closed lips an expression of amusement or pain.

"I'm Tom Claverack," he said, and half extended his hand. "Do you need a lift?" The preposterous redhead with the tilted fedora and yellow-green eyes took his hand in both of her gloves, looked up, and smiled.

"Thank you," she said. "My name iss Jenny Freuhoffer. You aaare ssso kind." The man pinched his grin very hard, paid his bill at the register, and took her bag from her. He held open the door of the diner and pointed to a slightly battered cream-colored sedan. While he put her bag in the trunk, Jenny got in the front seat, which was of creased white leather. Affixed to the middle of the dashboard was an ancient white papier-mâché duck with menacing yellow glass eyes, wearing a shot-glass-sized red tin fez.

AS HE DROVE, TOM CLAVERACK DID NOT LOOK DIRECTLY AT the girl's face, but he had a good view of her woolen lap on which hands twisted together, and of her skinny ankles. Still grinning his tight grin, he waited for her to talk. Three miles later, he gave in.

"Been to New York a lot?"

"No."

Silence. He looked away from the road at her face, the top half of which was concealed under the hat brim. Her blood-red mouth opened and a little cascade of laughter rattled out. Tom felt the sweat come up on his shoulders. He began scanning the sides of the highway for a turn-off where he could dump her. But then she spoke again, in a wispy baby voice.

"I am from Europe." It sounded like "fwum Eu-wop."

"Really? Where?"

"I was born in Chermany, but I went to school in Svitzerland. My parents are dead."

"A long time?"

"A year. Now I am living here."

"In New York?"

"Yes."

"What are you doing in Connecticut?"

"Where?"

"Here. How did you get here?"

"My mother's relatives live in Hartford. I vas visiting."

Tom strained to hear her soft voice. It seemed she had a problem with her r's. Or maybe she didn't. Maybe she was still just having problems with English. "Your English is very good," he ventured.

"I had good teachers." Jenny gazed out the window at the bright day, where the gas stations and office buildings set back from the highway shone white, not grey, white against the deep blue, with chrome and glass sending stabs of light into her eyes.

"In Switzerland?"

"Yes." Good, she thought, this is all coming out cool.

"Which school?"

"Ooh," she giggled. "I'm afraid I went to so many—they said I was, what is the word? Difficile. The boys—the drugs." Oh dear. That sounded dumb. Too nervous. Slow down.

"Did you go to Lausanne?"

"No, never there. But I had a cousin who did. She is"— the invention tumbled from her lips—"a skiing instructor."

"A student or a teacher?"

"Where," asked Jenny, "are ve now?"

"New Haven." He was looking at her lap. "You got into trouble with boys."

"Nothing very serious." Did she forget the accent? He made her nervous. "I haf never let it get too serious, you see." Was this a mistake? Would her prim claim make it worse, would he just stop looking at her like that? He turned on the radio. She sighed, a tiny sigh of relief that she turned into a cough.

A sinuous voice, banked by strings, came over the speakers: "The more I see you, the more . . ." The driver sang along, hamming it up, "My arms won't free you, my heart won't try."

Jenny looked at his face. She noticed his eyes for the first time: tucked in beneath heavy dark brows, they were alarmingly round and shiny, like a rodent's. And his unwrinkled face was oddly bulky, like a collection of smooth soft pouches, a couch covered with throw pillows. He looked happy. Was she going to be carsick? It was terrible; he was playing with *her.* But he was not playing very hard.

She looked past his head to the ocean in the distance, dotted with white things—boats or birds. Courage. "I lof American radio," she said loudly. "So much music. Do you haf a cigarette?"

"Sure. There's an old pack in the glove compartment, but it's stale." He reached over and popped the button, and a squashed red-and-white packet fell out. "I don't smoke anymore, but I like to keep them in case."

"In case?" Jenny extracted the matchbook from the cellophane wrapper, lit a match, and held it to the cigarette.

"In case I want one, then I can look at them, hold them in my hand, and not have one."

Jenny inhaled. "How Chermanic," she remarked. He laughed. Good. "You lif in New York?" she asked.

"Yes. Mostly."

"Is your house as nice as your car?" It came out sounding like an insult. Well, good.

"It's bigger."

"Where do you lif?"

"In the seventies, near Lexington Avenue."

Jenny put out her cigarette, then rolled down her window and spit out into the wind. She quickly rolled it back up. "What are the girls—the ladies—what are they vearing these days in New York?"

"Hats. They're wearing hats." He glanced at her fedora. "Not like that, though."

"Then what?"

"Big-brimmed Spanish hats, little red or navy pillboxes

draping veils, red skimmers, green tricorns, black fur things with earflaps, backwards baseball caps, every kind of hat you've ever seen." He paused to smirk. "Except like that."

Ignore it. "What else do zey wear?" Shit, not a z, that's French. "They vear?"

The driver looked as if he was going to laugh. But he struggled to keep his lips over his teeth. Jenny imagined his teeth were sharpened to points, like a rodent's. It didn't seem like a disgusting idea at all. What a mouth, she thought, and then felt a cold sick feeling pop in her gut. He moved his mouth, he was talking:

"The usual things. It changes all the time. It depends what part of town you're talking about, what circle." He liked the sound of his own voice. "But one thing remains, true as true—diamonds never go out of style." Jenny fleetingly wondered if he sold diamonds. "Otherwise it's too subtle for me. Except that plunging necklines are too L.A."

Jenny decided to lob him an easy one. "They do not dress—like me?"

Now he laughed, paternally. "You look fine. Besides, you're—European—so you could wear a garter belt and a burlap sack and you'd be avant-garde. . . . What—you'll be living downtown, something like that? East Village? You staying with friends?"

"I will be stopping at a hotel." She loved that verb. "What hotel can you recommend?"

"Nothing. Everything has gone downhill. But the Gramercy Park, maybe, or the Mayfair. . . . Once upon a time, you would have gone to the Barbizon, but everything changes. There's the Y, of course. . . ."

"What about the Plaza?"

"Recently purchased by an orangutan. Sure to go down."

"Eloise lived at the Plaza." Too late, she remembered that Eloise was not a real person, but a character in a book.

"Who?"

"A friend—of my mother's."

"Skip the Plaza."

"Does it still have the marble staircase, the fountain, the fat doorman?"

"So you've been there? Sure, it's all still there, but I hear from a very good source that they do not scald the pot for tea."

Jenny had no idea what he was talking about, but at least he was talking. She felt confident. "There are pigeons at the Plaza," she announced.

"Certainly." Now he looked confused.

"There are"—she paused dramatically—"pigeons in Berlin."

"Yes."

She laughed, not the little peal, but a low growly thing in her chest, so she sounded like a stage villain. Frank Sinatra's voice welled up from the radio: "In the wee small hours of the morning . . ." The clouds over the lowering sun thickened, and a grey light piled into the car. Jenny's nose got cold at the tip, and she pulled her hat down. More and more roads seemed to be converging and swarming beside the road they drove on, with more and more cars swiping close and trucks boxing them in. The head of the duck on the dashboard bobbed around in circles whenever the car changed lanes.

It was nearly four o'clock when they reached a tollbooth and a sort of highway bridge. The square empty towers of the city massed in front of them.

Jenny spoke. "What do they do with the garbage?"

III PIRATE JENNY III

Tom Claverack was startled out of a reverie. "They dump it in the ocean."

"That's horrible. They should bury it."

He ignored her. "So, where do you want to go, Fräulein?"

"The Plaza."

"Really?" He eyed her. "You wouldn't want to buy this car, would you? Kids like to have wheels in the city. Make you real popular . . . and it's always best to buy from a friend." His hand slid from the stick shift and lay next to her thigh.

Jenny moved and turned up the radio. "Hey," she said, "Peggy Lee!" He looked at her inquiringly, but she smiled at him, full force. "Vewy popular in Chermany," she assured him.

Tom found he had the hiccups. He took deep breaths to stop it, while the snarling blonde voice expressed the urgent desire that he get out of here and get her some money, too.

5

IT WAS ONLY BECAUSE SHE WAS SURE
the driver's eyes were on her back that Jenny was able to
climb the shallow steps of the Plaza. The sweat inside her
gloves made it difficult for her to grip the handle of her
suitcase. But she smiled at the doorman and waited while
he opened the door for her. The lobby was crowded with
people who were moving very quickly, and she got bumped
in the shoulder, then her suitcase was almost knocked out
of her hand, but she barely noticed. Almost immediately,
she knew that she should not be wearing the heavy makeup
on her eyes and mouth, and there was nothing she could do
about it. At least her clothes were not bulky. She thought of

the great uninhibited Eloise, lounging around on the back of a chair, brushing her hair in the elevator, running around the lobby in her socks. I feel more like Madeleine, thought Jenny. The sight of her black-cherry mouth in a mirrored pillar made her wipe it on her glove, hard, until it subsided to a mild rouge. But now one pale glove was stained as if with blood.

A woman at the reception desk calmly ignored her for a long time. Finally Jenny caught her eye.

"Could I speak to the manager?" That sounded official, very good.

"What for?" demanded the woman, whose milk-and-coffee skin and heavy burnished jewelry made all other skins and all other decorations look flashy.

Jenny spoke even more softly. "I would like to speak to the manager about a job."

The woman had lost interest. She looked down at some paperwork and said, "Take that door on your right and go downstairs. Talk to the woman at the desk."

A heavily carpeted staircase, like a rosy woolly hillside, sloped down to a long corridor of white walls and continuous pink carpet. The woman at the desk was much darker, much older, and almost kind. She asked Jenny what sort of job she was applying for. Jenny cleared her throat, but it came out as a whisper: "Hostess?" Somehow she imagined that hotels would have a hostess to show you to your room, the way the good restaurant in Chester had a hostess to show you to your table. But the woman looked scornful, and Jenny knew that this was not so.

"Maybe you want a domestic job?"

"I do not know." Very softly: "I am from Chermany."

She was handed a clipboard. "Fill that out. Leave it and

your résumé when you go. We'll call if something comes up." She stood and pointed a long pink nail at the bottom. "And don't forget references."

Jenny smelled defeat. She took the clipboard and filled it out in printing. Her brand-new name did not give her any pleasure. Her age she gave as twenty-three. She made up a birthday: March 11. But that was all. She approached the woman at the desk again. "Excuse me? I cannot fill this out. I do not haf a New York address yet, and no phone. And I don't have that"—she pointed dismally at the blanks.

"No social security number?"

Jenny nodded.

"You're from Germany? And you're an illegal? We can't hire people without a green card or alien registration, honey." Kindness took over from irritation. "Do you know what that is?"

Jenny shook her head and bit her lip. She decided that tears would be a good idea; they seemed to be coming anyway. They did, rolling fat ones.

"Oh my goodness," said the woman. She grabbed a tissue. "Here. Maybe you can wipe off some of that stuff while you're at it."

"Thank you," sniffed Jenny, blotting carefully but by no means removing her lashes. She honked once. The woman picked up the phone receiver and punched.

"Peter, honey? It's Allison. Unh hunh, oh yes." She laughed, then raised her brows at Jenny. "Hang on, I'm going to take this in the next room." She pushed a button and the light blinked, while she disappeared into a cubicle and shut the door. Jenny considered picking up the extension but decided it was too risky.

Almost immediately, Allison was back in her chair. She

wrote on a piece of scrap paper. "Now you go down the block here, to the Addams Hotel, see, and you ask for Mr. Calhoun. I think"—she lowered her voice—"he can maybe give you a job. It won't be minimum-wage, but it's all cash, you know, off the books. They have a big turnover—and they prefer *white* slavery. Now don't tell anyone else." Jenny opened her eyes big and shook her head. She stared at the piece of paper. "Don't worry," Allison laughed. "It's a nice place."

"What is CPS?"

"That's Central Park South, honey, Fifty-ninth Street, you're *on* it! Good Lord, *right* off the turnip truck, aren't we? Go back outside and down the front steps, then turn *left,* and it's down in the middle of the second block. It's got a green awning."

The lobby was even noisier and brighter than before. Jenny was bumped out among a herd of furs. As she turned left and started walking, she saw the trees ahead and realized that she was looking at Central Park. South. Right. There was a moment of panic: Would she run into Gail Hinzmann, her mother's friend? No; that was ridiculous, another city. Besides, even though the street was jammed with people, no one looked her in the eye. The buildings were taller than the buildings in Boston, she was sure of it. But the park looked dark and restful. She regained her courage.

After she found the awning, which was ribbed like an umbrella, she hesitated. It was the right number, but there was no name, just a smooth wooden door with a brass handle. The door was shaped like a huge keyhole, with scallops running along the wood frame. Jenny leaned on the handle and pushed. There was a long narrow lobby, tiled in blue and green and yellow mosaic stars, and in the middle of the tiles, like a miniature swimming pool, a flat square of water with a bubble of spitting liquid in the middle. Tall ferns and plants with big, paddle-shaped leaves made everything smell like earth. A tall narrow blond man hurried toward her. "Yes?"

"Mr. Calhoun?"

"Oh. No. I spoke to him. In there."

Past the elevators, down another narrow, tiled corridor, Jenny pushed in another keyhole door, and found an office whose inhabitant was a young, fair-haired man with horn-rimmed glasses, clad in what looked like a garage mechanic suit of light grey tweed. He sat in an armchair, an open file of papers on his lap, and Jenny saw that what she had, at first startled glance, taken to be blood pouring from his throat was instead an unknotted silky bow tie. She tried again. "Mr. Calhoun?"

"Ah. The girl."

Shit, she thought. He's English. And my accent is terrible; he'll know. She decided to mumble.

"You know that we need a chambermaid right this minute? We're got unexpected parties arriving right now and the place on five is a shambles. Can you just start? You've done this before—?"

Jenny was far too cowed for her prepared line: I haf cleaned the finest hotels in Euwop. So she just nodded instead.

"Go get Peter. He'll show you. He'll give you a get-up, and we *do* insist on the apron and the mob cap at all times. God knows, we don't want the guests to see you at all, but should they do so, you smile. Now go get Peter." He waved her off.

III   PIRATE JENNY   III

Peter was not, perhaps, as helpful as he might have been, but within fifteen minutes she was mopping a toilet and cleaning a mirror and wiping crumbs into the radiator vent in 5A-B, one of the establishment's ten demi-suites. There were also, she was to learn, five full suites and thirty regular rooms. Eventually she was joined by another maid, Loua, who spelled her name and explained she was an actor.

Together they worked until midnight, in a hurried, edgy way, barely one step ahead of returning guests. When they turned back the black-and-green embroidered bed covers, which Jenny thought looked like tablecloths, they placed a foil-wrapped mint and a desiccated black olive side by side on each pillow. "It's part of the Spanish-Moorish motif," Loua explained. "I think it's a ghastly idea, but Peter doesn't take too well to criticism, if you know what I mean, and you *will* know what I mean." She moved her face a lot as she talked, in the manner of a clown, but she wasn't particularly funny. Jenny decided it was because her voice was flat. But she didn't mind listening. The questions about Germany she silenced by saying, "My parents died just last year. I don't want to talk about it, okay?" This worked well—no doubt in part because Loua wasn't really interested anyway—but Jenny was pleased. She could use it again.

As they disrobed after midnight in the employee bathroom on the mezzanine, Jenny tentatively asked Loua where she should go for the night.

"You mean you don't have anyplace to go? Well, you know, it's not that I don't *want* you or anything, but I've already got two roommates, and everything. You could go to the Y."

"Where is that?"

"Actually, you know—this is risky, but I did it once when my old boyfriend was lurking at my apartment and I couldn't go home—he had the key—well, I could have gone home but I wouldn't give him the satisfaction, and I just wasn't up for a full-scale limited nuclear attack, if you know what I mean. I stayed here."

"In the bathroom?"

"No. In a room. There's two rooms on the second floor empty tonight, late cancellations. It's very dicey because Peter—he's practically round the clock, you know?—and the maid shift in the morning—Lily is all right but Eileen and Mrs. Caton are pigs—but you just have to dodge 'em and be out by six. Peter won't be on duty till eight."

So Jenny spent her first night in New York lying fully clothed on top of a bedspread, hardly able to breathe, let alone sleep. But she dozed, while outside the roar of the city, the tires and the engines and the door slamming and the voices, came at her like a dark wave filled with detritus, a dark and populated ocean that could carry her out with it, through the slats in the Venetian blinds, out onto the bricks and into the alley, then washed out onto the streets where everyone was swimming or drowning, she couldn't tell yet.

THE NEXT MORNING JENNY PUT HER SUITCASE IN THE HOTEL basement behind some boxes and then slipped out into the street by seven-thirty. It was chilly, and she had no idea where she was going. Except for juice and crackers and a tinfoil triangle of soft cheese from the room's refrigerator, she had not eaten in a long time. She walked steadily westward, then south a couple of blocks, until she found a suitably shabby coffee shop. After spending an astonishing amount on scrambled eggs and toast, she drank a second

III PIRATE JENNY III

cup of coffee and pondered. Her new black flat shoes were already wearing at the heel. She would not be paid until next week.

The day was spent in walking, walking around the several blocks east and west and behind the hotel. Jenny felt like a detective, or a spy; she would play a game of walking a block, then trying to recall the name of every storefront, in order. Or the color and style of every car parked along the way. She knew this was aimless, but she believed that she was getting practice.

When she cleaned that night, she ate the room-service leavings when Loua wasn't looking: toast crusts, half a banana, an egg salad sandwich from a plate where a cigarette had died an early death. That night she spent down in the basement near her suitcase, on a couple of foam pillows she'd snatched from a room. It was a relief to sleep without fear, and she slept deeply. The next day she ate only coffee and toast for breakfast, and then in the midafternoon she returned to the hotel, too tired to keep walking. Peter stopped her in the lobby and reminded her that she wasn't due until six. But she said she had left something behind, and went up a flight to the mezzanine. She sat on the floor of the ladies' room and rested, her back against the hard silver curves of the radiator, then realized after dozing for about twenty minutes that Peter would be on the lookout. She'd have to leave. She fixed her face (no eyeliner, blotted lipstick) and then wearily opened the door, as she did bumping into a little, dapper man in a gray suit with a face like a frog.

"Hey!" he said. "Watch where you're going!"

"Sorry." She looked down.

"You on staff?"

"What?"

"Are you one of the maids?"

"Oh. Yes." She looked up, and did a half-smile.

"Listen." He placed a hand confidingly on her shoulder, and brought his face much too close in toward hers. He fished out his wallet. "Think you could do me a little favor?" He displayed a twenty-dollar bill. It had better be little, Jenny thought. "Could you give Mr. Cooms's suite a touch-up, honey? Just the bed, you know, and the bath. And we don't have to tell anyone about it."

Jenny took the bill. "Where is it?"

"On six. You must be new."

"Yes." Jenny practiced her new way of talking very slow, each word elaborately enunciated. All very soft. No funny consonants. "I am very new. I do not know Mr. Cooms."

"Ha. Well. Never mind. You just hurry along."

"Thank you, Mr.—?"

"Herb. But we don't talk about it, right?"

"No, Mr. Herb."

He laughed and vanished into the stairwell. Jenny took the elevator up to six, and tried her passkey in the only door without a number, the full suite at the front. Inside, it was more of an apartment than a hotel room. Although the architecture was mosaicked and scalloped like the rest of the hotel, Mr. Cooms had overlain it with a personal style—what Jenny thought of as "modern"—black metal lamps that looked like dental instruments, a black-and-white mottled cow-skin rug on the green tiled floor, big confusing paintings on the walls. The bedroom was fairly disheveled, she guessed by Herb and a friend. She changed the sheets and cleaned up the glasses and ice. The bathroom had a bigger tub than any of the other rooms in the hotel, and it was currently lined with a lavender foam that proved oily and resistant to the scrubbing sponge.

||| PIRATE JENNY |||

That evening she asked Loua about Mr. Cooms. He owned the hotel, it seemed, with Mr. Belman. Mr. Cooms was in jail, it was ridiculous, a tax fraud but someone in the DA's office had singled him out as an example. No one knew why Mr. Belman wasn't in jail, too.

"So his suite is empty?" Jenny asked innocently.

"Well, not during the trial it wasn't. I mean, *everyone* famous came and stayed in the Addams and went and testified as character witnesses or just to lend moral support, you know? But Mr. Cooms went to Allenwood, like, 'I Was a Prisoner on a Golf Course,' in June and he'll be there eighteen months, or twelve with good behavior. I think."

"Who is Herb?"

"That's Mr. Belman."

"Does he live here too?"

"No, he's got that chateau in Connecticut, exact replica, you know, with that wife, the one nobody will invite. He hangs around the hotel a lot lately." Loua paused and pushed her dark bangs out of her eyes. "Watch your butt, if you know what I mean, with Mr. Belman, and you *will* know what I mean."

How delightful. Jenny moved into Mr. Cooms's suite, and resolved to lie as low as she could. She hid her suitcase in the kitchenette and cleaned the place obsessively after herself. A couple of days later, as she was coming onto her six-P.M. shift, Herb pulled her aside and told her to tidy the room again.

Jenny smiled. "Mr. Herb?"

"What?"

"Perhaps you would prefer . . ." Slow down, slow. "I could check on the room every afternoon, late, and if it needs to be cleaned, you could just leave me the money?"

Herb blinked a couple of times. "Smart girl." He patted

her bottom. "Smart girl." He pinched, lightly. Jenny pretended not to notice.

Herb's afternoon liaisons, Jenny discovered, involved three different women. One, an elegant black brunette with huge eyes and enormous, missilelike breasts, she was pretty sure Herb paid. Another woman—petite, white, timid, expensively dressed—gave Herb money and presents. Jenny thought that was all until the second week she was at the hotel, when one afternoon she was alarmed to hear Herb at the door. Fortunately, the bed was made, and she scrambled into the closet, closed the door, and wedged the lock shut from the inside with a towel.

Herb's companion did not speak. They grunted hurriedly together, then the woman went into the bathroom and locked the door. Herb knocked sternly, then called out, then timidly tapped, but she did not open the door until after he had gone. The woman dressed quickly—and Jenny got a glimpse of a broad rear end going out the door.

The wall of stereo and television and video equipment that graced Mr. Cooms's bedroom gave Jenny ideas about taping Herb and then blackmailing him. The prospect made her chuckle; she rubbed her hands together like a comic villain and wished she had a friend to laugh about this with. But this time she had to be her own killjoy; she knew it was too dangerous. "Recognize your limitations," she repeated to herself. Where did that nugget of wisdom come from? Not from the Dads, surely.

Besides, there were so many other bits and pieces of opportunities in the Addams. Mr. Cooms had generously installed one significant device: a TV monitor that observed the front door of the lobby. Jenny watched as the guests came and went, reduced to bent black-and-white forms, with enormous heads and shoulders tapering away to tiny little feet: the businessmen and their wives, from L.A.; the Japanese men who traveled in packs; and the English ones, dozens and dozens of them, in their goofy outfits and slouched shoulders, boys wearing makeup, girls with shorn heads. Some of them were musicians, at least that was the official word, and Jenny once did have to clean dried cola and rib sauce off an electric keyboard. In her observations at the monitor, she learned two things: that most people leave a little spot at the back of their hair unbrushed; and that most couples head out for the evening quarreling.

From their rooms she promptly inferred that English people are the filthiest in the world, followed closely by the French. But there was a dividend: the loot. Confronted with a dressing table bestrewn with jewelry, and a floor thick with suitcases that dripped scarves and belts and shirts, Jenny felt reasonably comfortable lifting an item here and there. How would the owner miss it? She acquired a delicate pair of earrings, little golden chains with three golden balls, the size of ball bearings, suspended on the ends. She lifted a pale spring-green silk chiffon scarf, a red lizard belt, and, from an especially messy Brazilian painter, a manicure kit that was already missing the nail file.

Larger thefts worried her, but she found a good method. The night before one couple—the female half of which happened to have her exact shoe size—departed from the Addams, Jenny slipped into their room. She took the coveted dark green suede shoes, with pointy toes and Cuban heels, and tucked them on the top closet shelf, behind the extra bed pillows. She waited a long forty-eight hours after their departure; and then the shoes were hers.

A French journalist, a woman with a glossy red mouth and long silky sideburns of hair, presented a great temptation—her belongings were wonderful—but Jenny did not dare steal from her, because everything was too neatly arranged. But as she gazed at the top tray of her jewelry box, she saw a pair of earrings, incredible earrings, pear-shaped pearls that hung from ruby-studded shields. So she stole one. After about a week, she took to wearing it like a brooch on the collar of her blouse. One day it got wet in the rain and then dried next to a heater and the skin of the pearl came off and Jenny realized it was plastic and threw it away.

But every night there were clean, crisp sheets, and a long, perfumed bath. Jenny was usually too tired to watch television—except in the afternoon, but then she was too wary for the sound of Herb's key in the lock. As she became more confident of Herb's habits, she felt able to sleep a little later in the morning, watching the monitor for Peter to go out for his ten-o'clock coffee—at which point she would quietly leave the hotel for the day, just like a guest.

She had been working at the Addams for two and a half weeks when she found some tickets in the pocket of a man's jacket hanging in the closet of demi-suite 4 A-B. They were for the fall antiques show. Since the man had ten tickets, Jenny took two and invited Peter to come with her. This was not her first such overture. She had already shared her last remaining joint with him, up on the roof one night, and had succeeded in thawing him out. He was impressed by the news that she was German; she told him that she was from a noble family that had lost all its money, and that she had gone to college in the U.S. He didn't ask many questions, but talked a lot about himself—his boyfriends and the plays they attended, and the concerts, and his old friend who was in the hospital. He was such a funny mixture of the sophisticated—always finding sexual innuendo that mystified Jenny, or referring to famous people by their first names—

and the naive, his feelings so easily hurt, his knowledge of women hopelessly circumscribed by a devotion to glamour. On that night, and on other nights, over coffee, sometimes over a bottle of wine from Mr. Calhoun's office, Jenny let him talk.

Peter was delighted about the antiques show. Jenny knew better than to feign knowledge with him; instead she said she knew nothing about the field, but wanted to educate herself. So Peter got to be in charge, took her elbow and swept her through into the Armory on 62nd Street, beneath the banners and past the dragons at the door. He was wearing the glasses that he thought made him look serious, but that struck Jenny as comical, like glasses on a giraffe. He steered her to the fanciest collection of clocks she had ever seen: a mantelpiece clock with intricate golden shepherdesses and shepherds inclined toward a dense, slightly stippled crystal that turned the face of the clock pale purple; a pocket watch with the phases of the moon leering in the center of the dial; a squat clock like a teakettle that played Russian folk songs at the half hour; an ogreish grandfather clock with a pendulum the size of a small brass pizza.

Leaving Peter to talk with the clock dealer, Jenny wandered down an aisle. She watched the men and woman who moved among the dealers, exclaiming in modulated, almost inaudible glee at the cupboards, the rugs, the desks, the lamps, the odds and ends, the china and glassware and paintings: "Henry, look. Didn't we see that at—?" "No, dear, it's not exactly like it, see the beveling on the . . .?" Or: "Perfectly lovely, of course, if you like that sort of thing." Or: "Betsy's mother must have *five* of these." Or: "I can't *stand* it, it's *per*fect, *what* do you want to bet it's at least twenty?"

Jenny wandered past dealers who sold only quilts, only lampshades, only yellow glass, or odd combinations—one sold duck decoys and Chinese plates. At a surreptitious distance, she followed one quiet, well-dressed man for about twenty minutes. Then, carefully imitating his manner, she would go to a case and stare for a while at some small, inexplicable item in ivory or porcelain or stone or leather or wood, then ask the dealer if she could see it. He would unlock the glass case and hand her the object—which would turn out to be a bejeweled snuffbox, a carved watch fob, an old button, a prayer book. Jenny would turn the object over in her hands, memorizing it, and then sometimes ask the price. Whatever it was, she would keep fingering the object that now burned in her hand for another minute before handing it back with a small, but by no means rueful, smile. "Thank you." No one seemed to know she had no money. Maybe, she thought, it's my new suede shoes.

A celluloid cigarette holder, in transparent imitation tortoiseshell, was made in the 1930s and cost $125. I should have gotten one at the flea market, thought Jenny, as she handed it back to the dealer.

ONE NIGHT AT WORK LOUA ASKED JENNY IF SHE WAS INTERested in a one-shot job. "It's this acting troupe I work with sometimes—a couple of the guys do parties, you know, for children, and they asked me if I'd come with them and I said yes. But then I learned that they only wanted me to be a sort of helper, chaperon the kids, you know, and that's pretty unprofessional as well as insulting, and I told them to forget it. But now they're stuck and it's a Halloween party so it's Thursday. You want to do it? It's just a couple of hours and you just have to watch the kids and make sure they don't drown when they bob for apples or something. Some Park Avenue place. Thirty bucks."

"No tip?"

"You'll have to figure that out with the guys. Sure."

"Okay."

"Here's the name—Mrs. Washburn. And Bill's number, too."

6

HALLOWEEN IN NEW YORK, IT SEEMED, did not mean silly shy children with makeup and plastic masks and long capes dragging on the ground. It did not mean shopping bags and orange candy peanuts, and certainly not caramel apples and burning leaves. Mrs. Washburn's children's party, hosted on behalf of her seven-year-old, Gemma, was a somewhat formal affair; the big orange invitations said "Three P.M. Prompt!" Jenny arrived an hour early, rendezvoused with Bill and his two acting buddies in the kitchen, and got going with the decorations, under Mrs. Washburn's martial hand.

Hastily they opened blue-and-gilt paper boxes of lumpy chocolate-chip cookies, and tissue-wrapped bags of orange- and black-coated candy almonds. The almonds went into glass bowls, the cookies went on glass platters, and Jenny was mixing orange punch in a big glass pitcher before she realized what was bothering her: no paper plates! But Mrs. Washburn appeared unconcerned, stacking elegant tiny punch glasses with hollow handles. Jenny imagined every single handle snapping off.

Dozens of miniature pumpkins had already been wired together like outsize cherry clusters. With black and orange velvet ribbon, Jenny tied these into festoons that bunched at the bases of the foyer chandelier and the wall brackets in the dining room. One of Bill's buddies was enlisted to start the fire in the foyer, as Jenny artfully piled more pumpkins and members of related squash families in corners and on the table.

Mrs. Washburn and the actors disappeared to the separate toilettes, and Jenny was left alone to snitch cookies and talk to the butler, a rather rotund elderly black man—clad, very much to his evident annoyance, in a satin Satan suit. Jenny made him feel better by tucking the tail up at his waist and by agreeing with him that he could remove the gloves with the two-inch red nails and it wouldn't matter.

The guests were indeed prompt, arriving with mothers or baby-sitters in tow. The butler greeted each child with his party favor, a bright papier-mâché animal mask. Jenny helped with the business of tying the masks onto the children's faces. Mrs. Washburn and her husband, a tall man, appeared in costume—she as a sort of queen with tiara fixed to a towering white wig and big beauty spot on her cheek, he as Abraham Lincoln. Several of the smaller children screamed when they saw them. About twenty children all told clustered in groups of two or three in the dining room and foyer, comparing animal faces. The older ones pushed their masks back on their heads like knights taking a breather from the battle, and got busy shoving one another's masks back down. Some masks apparently lacked eyeholes; one little tiger fell blindly over a pumpkin and swore, bizarrely: "Mister Tree-Fucker." Mothers and baby-sitters smirked.

Just then, from the kitchen, Bill and his friends swept in, painted green all over, hideously hung about with rags and wearing little else but mud-brown jockstraps. They carried a lobster pot, which they set down in the middle of the carpet and danced around, hollering "Double, double, toil and trouble," and "Fair is foul, and foul is fair, hover through fog and filthy air." The screaming started anew, and two children were carried off to the bathroom. Bill rubbed his hands together and continued to his cowering audience: "Eye of newt, and toe of frog, wool of bat, and tongue of dog." Mrs. Washburn, with a fierce smile on her face, removed the lobster pot and nearly shouted, "Refreshments!" while one of the bigger girls kept repeating, "Tongue of dog! Tongue of dog! Are we eating tongue of dog?"

Smelling what could very well have been scorching squash, Jenny positioned herself in front of the fireplace in the hall and nervously pressed her lipsticked lips together. Mr. Washburn tipped his head to get the stovepipe hat under the doorjamb and joined her.

"How's it going? Which kids are yours?"

Speak slow. "I'm here with the actors. Just to help." She smiled bravely.

"Is that an accent?"

"I am from Germany, yes."

"Really? Hey, listen. Ich bin ein Hamburger!" He laughed.

Jenny smiled and showed her teeth. "I only speak English now," she said. "To learn. Full immersion."

"Great, you're doing great." Mr. Washburn looked serious and told Jenny about his eldest daughter, whose name sounded something like Bushy, top ten of her class at Brearley. She'd gone to one of those intensive language-study things in Avignon, France, last summer, spoke French like a native now. She could join the diplomatic corps, you never know, but her mother, who lived in Virginia, was pushing for international public relations, and he could see her point. "Interesting thing," he continued, as his Abe-beard fell away from his left sideburn, "how these backyard countries will do an ad campaign to build confidence with foreign investors. . . ."

Jenny stared into the dining room as one girl, egged on by two boys, snuck up behind another girl and pulled her tights and panties down to her knees. An opera of screams issued from the room, but Mr. Washburn kept on talking. Jenny had to put a hand on his baggy forearm and say firmly, "Excuse me, the children," and, smiling sweetly, walk into the fray. The victim meanwhile hiked up her drawers and tried to kick the other girl's shins, but missed and kicked a table instead. Jenny saved the table from toppling, then took the little girl's hand and drew her off to one side. Gazing at the sulky face, Jenny guessed she was about nine.

"What's your name?" she asked, because she couldn't think of anything else to say. The girl was struggling under Jenny's grip on her shoulders, but she answered: "Shelley."

"Is your mother here, Shelley?"

The child fixed her with a look of capacious scorn. "She is in Buenos Aires," she said.

"Your baby-sitter?"

But Shelley pulled herself away and almost ran through the dining room into another part of the house. Jenny was relieved to see the butler head after and retrieve her, because meanwhile Gemma and a little boy with a fixed grin on his face were discovering that the melted chocolate from the chips in the cookies made a kind of lipstick. Jenny thought she'd have to interfere and this time was joined by a fleet of mothers and baby-sitters, all with dampened napkins and hankies for cleaning up. Finally, at four-thirty, the butler rang a cowbell and everyone filed into the hall. The butler handed each escort a small silver box of Belgian chocolates and let them out. The actors promptly left as well. While the butler ferried the party's leavings into the kitchen, Jenny tackled the cleaning up. She shooed the still-bewigged Mrs. Washburn away from the sink and washed the dishes herself while the hostess idly collected ribbons and other trash into a heap on the countertop and complained about the children—how they were all so spoiled, how that awful Robert was always making her dear Gemma silly like that—well, she wasn't sure but a little boy who wants to put on lipstick was *not* something she would turn a blind eye to if she were his mother! Jenny giggled appreciatively. Four punch-glass handles had, in fact, broken; Jenny watched with amazement as Mrs. Washburn simply tossed them into the trash without a word.

She would be late for work—but Mrs. Washburn pressed a five-dollar tip into her hand as she left, so that was something.

Back at the hotel, Loua told her that Peter had left for the evening, dressed in green tights and a tunic, for the down-

III PIRATE JENNY III

town Halloween parade. "Is he Peter Pan, then?" asked Jenny. "No, that's what I thought, but he's Mary Martin *as* Peter Pan."

One afternoon Jenny went to the movies on Third Avenue and treated herself afterwards to tea at the Plaza. She had not been back there since that first night, and she felt unreasonably frightened, as if someone would recognize her. She brought a glossy magazine and forced herself to lean back, in an imitation of calm leisure, into the armchair she was shown—off to one side behind a tall fern in a figured blue pot. She leafed through the magazine with elaborate unconcern and tried not to fumble when the waitress asked her what kind of tea she would like. One was a breakfast tea, and Jenny shook her head, smiling, thinking that she'd avoided a terrible faux pas; one was unpronounceable; so she wound up choosing Earl Grey—and cucumber sandwiches, which seemed traditional. When the pot arrived, she touched it, found it cool, and, remembering the sneer of the man who had given her the ride, looked around the Palm Court for other signs of deterioration. But she knew so little—perhaps the lamination on the menus was tacky. Or maybe the china itself—little violets strewn over white—was wrong. She really had no idea. And she couldn't see well enough to judge the other patrons, since she was virtually imprisoned behind the fern. After half a cup, the cooling tea tasted funny, like perfume. Feeling very like a movie, she poured the rest into the fern when no one was looking. The cucumber sandwiches were fine; she was somewhat chagrined to realize that they tasted exactly like what you'd expect slices of cucumber between white bread with mayonnaise to taste like. Leaving the magazine, she drifted toward the ladies' room and then out to 59th

Street by a side door. Jenny did not think tea should cost seventeen dollars.

At work, Loua was all fired up with a message: Jenny should call Mrs. Washburn about a job. No, not another party, some sort of live-in baby-sitting. Jenny was not very interested, and said so. But Loua went on: "It might be really right for you, because it's room and board—you still don't have an apartment, right?—so it's a whole lot cheaper than the Y. And board is food, so there's that. And I think it's with you know like a big important family, and you're illegal-alien status, right? So they could help you get legal. It happens all the time."

Privately, Jenny discounted this last idea. But she agreed to look into it. Bill had left Mrs. Washburn's number, so Jenny called and was set up to meet a Mrs. Kovalenko at her home the next day.

"They're desperate," said Jenny after hanging up. "Their baby-sitter just quit. It's for their grandchildren."

"Oooh," said Loua. "Maybe you could get more money."

"You think so?" said Jenny, opening her eyes wide and looking doubtful.

A sturdy midsized housekeeper answered the door at the posh row house on East 73rd Street. She was wearing an over-the-head apron but otherwise appeared to be dressed in normal clothes. Jenny had worn her uniform from the Addams, to look more professional, but now felt silly. She considered keeping her long raincoat—a hand-me-down from Peter—on. "Let me take your coat," said the woman, and plucked it off her back. She gave Jenny's outfit a look. "Upstairs, one flight." Jenny snatched off the mob cap with its lace frill and handed it to her with the coat. The woman seemed reluctant to take it.

"Would you please put that with my coat?" She spoke even more slowly than usual. Looking as though she could say something but wouldn't, the woman complied.

Jenny immediately liked the feel of the house: heavy, old, dark, comfortable. It was not cheerful, but cheer seemed unnecessary where there was so much comfort. She waded through a dark carpet to the stairs and climbed, as if through crimson snow, to the second floor. It was one big room, the whole floor, with windows on either end and a long blond wood floor running its length. There were paintings on the white walls, dark paintings in lumpy golden frames. It looked exactly like a museum, except for the couch and chairs and elaborate carved desk that clustered near the front windows. The desk was mobbed with papers, behind which sat a small, elderly woman, like a gnome. Her hair was blonde and wound up in a bun at the back of her head, her mouth was a brilliant orange pink line, and her cheeks were rouged and powdered. She raised a long monkey arm with a long curled claw and waved to Jenny, bracelets rattling. Jenny approached as she was bidden. Mrs. Kovalenko's feet did not touch the floor. She looked very old—in her eighties, probably. But she spoke with perfect clarity, in a beautiful, violinlike voice:

"You want this chob?"

Oh my God, thought Jenny, is she German? "I do not know."

"Speak up, I'm not deaf, but speak up."

"What would the job be?" she asked, louder, but still very slow. She tucked her black skirt under her ass and sat down on the edge of the couch. Now she was shorter than the old woman.

"Live in, mind the children. Take them to school, play with them, make sure they eat dinner."

"How many children?"

"Two," she said, crossly, as if it was obvious. "My grand-children. Their parents are away, and they live with us. Mrs. Hayworth is busy enough, and little Juanita had to return to Costa Rica. She *says* her mother is ill." Then Mrs. Kovalenko made a noise that sounded exactly like "Bah!"

Jenny cleared her throat. "Where were you born?"

Mrs. Kovalenko spent a long moment looking offended before saying, as if she were speaking to the stupidest person she had ever met, "Russia." The R rolled.

"I am from Germany," said Jenny slowly.

The woman smiled. "It does not matter," she said forgivingly. "I do not mind, but you speak only English with the children, of course. We will make an exception for your charming lullabies, of course." Jenny had no idea what she meant, but she smiled hopefully. "And you speak French, of course." Jenny was silent, smiling.

"It's two hundred a week, room and board," Mrs. Kovalenko said abruptly. Jenny frowned, although this was more than her salary at the Addams. She would be losing the steady income from Mr. Belman.

"All right, two hundred and fifty. I need references."

"I can get the manager at the hotel . . ." Jenny paused, then plunged artfully. "But I am otherwise friendless. My parents are dead, my relatives in Germany are impoverished. But I have a good education." That wasn't enough. She smiled. "And I love children."

Mrs. Kovalenko hopped out of her chair and stood impatiently by the side of her desk. "Leave your phone number, and the number of the hotel manager."

Shyly, Jenny looked at her hands. "I have no number, I am at the Y."

"The what?"

"The Y. But here is the number of my reference. I will call you tomorrow."

The old woman picked up the phone and Jenny left. She lurked for a moment on the landing, then realized that the call was to a drugstore, not Peter, so she headed back down the stairs. Her coat and cap were in the closet next to the front door, and she could hear what was presumably Mrs. Hayworth, talking or singing in the kitchen. She let herself out.

FOR THE NEXT TWO DAYS, THE BUZZ AT THE ADDAMS WAS OF Mr. Cooms's application for parole. Jenny carefully kept her face neutral, but she was interested to see that everyone—Mr. Calhoun, Peter, the maids, and especially, it seemed, Mr. Belman—was none too pleased with the idea of Mr. Coom's return. To her mild surprise, but very real relief, Jenny got the new job.

She was to begin the following Monday, but went to the house to meet the children on Saturday. When she saw who the children were—the little girl who'd been debagged at the party and the littler boy with the bizarre cursing vocabulary—she almost decided not to do it after all. But in their grandmother's presence the two were demure, almost mute, as the old woman recited the prominent facts about the family like a lesson that Jenny should memorize. She and her husband were White Russians (Jenny would have to ask Peter if he knew what that meant) and had emigrated in 1917—"I was a child." Their son, Nicholas, and his wife, Carla, were abroad on business. When the old woman left her alone with the children, the girl vanished to her own room and the boy patiently told Jenny that she should watch him while he played with Evil Raiders—which turned out to be plastic dinosaurs that drove long low cars and helicopters and vans, conveniently equipped with Mortal Death Rays. The boy's name was Keats—and his grandmother, in her return to the room, observed to Jenny in a tart aside that she wondered if, in naming her offspring Shelley and Keats, their mother might have been mistaking them for a pair of cats. As it happened, she went on, Isolde—the twenty-year-old daughter of Nicholas's first marriage, who was away at college—had come up with the modified Keaton, which everyone but the boy's mother now used. And one more thing: Nicholas, Carla, and the children had the discreetly shortened last name of Koval. The old woman wedged her mouth as if she were going to spit.

Jenny enjoyed Mrs. Kovalenko's gossip at the expense of her descendants. It boded well.

And so she moved in. The children called their grandmother Netta, and their grandfather was called Nikki. Tiny like his wife, Nikki shuffled in and out of the elevator to come to the dining room for meals, but otherwise spent the whole day in his study on the third floor—drowsing, apparently. He did not acknowledge Jenny's presence, which made her very nervous.

The room they put Jenny in was not on the top, fourth floor—where the housekeeper occupied an apartment with a rather grand setup of her own—but a tight little room in the cellar, with over-the-head casement windows that faced south into the garden. The cement walls had been painted a bright yellow and the effect was actually sunny. The bed was comfortable, she had a lovely old, only slightly battered, dark wood dresser and a dressing table, and an easy chair, and—most important—her own bathroom, with a shower. One of the first games Jenny played with Keaton was to have him go down to her room and scream as loud as he could while she stood upstairs by the basement door—first with it open, then with it closed—and moving about the first floor of the house. When the basement door was closed, no sound was audible in the main part of the house. This was privacy.

Of course, she did not get much time alone. Shelley and Keaton were in Jenny's care from the first thing in the morning through breakfast, and she walked them the ten-block round trip to their schools. Until about three in the afternoon, she assisted Mrs. Hayworth: doing laundry, cleaning, marketing. Then the children were picked up after school, escorted by foot or taxi to lessons and friends—then entertained, bathed, and bedded down.

Jenny was amazed by how little a seven-year-old boy and a nine-year-old girl have in common, but at least that made it easier to break up their fights. Except the ones about their mother and father. Shelley liked to announce where they were—no longer in Buenos Aires, it seemed, but now in Caracas, on business that involved paintings. But whenever Shelley went on for too long speculating about what they were eating, or the weather, or whatever else she had learned from postcards and phone calls, Keaton would hold his hands over his ears and rock and cry—or else resort to his favorite tactic, biting. He often bit Jenny as well, so it was prudent to shut him in his room at the first sign of gnashing.

Apart from Saturday afternoons, which the children often spent with the families of friends in the park, the only time Jenny could be sure of time to herself was on Sunday afternoons. Then their grandmother hustled them out in full regalia to the waiting car which rolled them majestically to St. Nicholas's Cathedral, for a mass that lasted more than two hours. It was a Christian blessing, those two hours, after all.

To Jenny's surprise, Thanksgiving was easy—the Kovalenkos did not believe in it, and instead took the children to a restaurant. Furthermore, Jenny got both Thursday and Friday off, as did Mrs. Hayworth, because their employers confused it with Labor Day—and so treated the holiday with a disdainful, dreadful formality.

Jenny spent Friday afternoon with Peter. He filled her in on the latest at the Addams. Mr. Cooms had *not* gotten parole. Mr. Calhoun and Mr. Belman had been arguing over money, and Peter was worried about his job. Very carefully, in great detail, Jenny told him about Mr. Belman's afternoons. Peter already knew about the black woman and made a guess about the silent visitor. But his eyes popped comically as Jenny described the small woman. "Mrs. Stokes!" he gurgled. "Oh my *God. Thank* you." "Noblesse oblige," Jenny replied, because she thought it meant "No obligation, on the house."

Jenny told him all about her Russians—the gallery of paintings, the enormous dining-room table that looked like something out of a medieval castle, the heavy dark draperies, the mysterious old man who lived upstairs. She made it sound like a story by Edgar Allan Poe.

But she did not tell him about the times, late at night, when she woke from crying, or with a shout from a nightmare. How she would stand on her dressing table and stare out the window into the back garden, where maybe a little moonlight made the dead leaves on the bushes and the iron chairs and the cement fountain look silvery and far away, how she would plug in her earphones and listen to her cassettes—usually *Die Dreigroschenoper*—in German that she would never understand but had always known. How her own voice had become these lost, bitter voices, how her no doubt imminent triumph was identical with her despair.

After coffee with Peter, she walked north along the Park, shivering despite the two sweaters under her flapping raincoat. Stepping on the hexagonal honeycomb of stones that was lined with leaves and wrappers, she didn't see the ice. She fell hard on her rear, and just sat there. A man walking by offered to help her up but she was laughing so hard he couldn't understand a word she said.

7

JENNY WAS WAKENED IN THE MORNING
by lines of sun on her face, a sea of yellow that crashed
against the walls. She felt a suffocated shock, and turned
violently about in the bed. Breathing heavily, she yanked
the covers to one side, in search of the dark, dreaming version of herself, wearing her old plaid knickers and plain
brown hair curled back from her face. Once, frightened by
a similar hallucination, Jenny had lurched from the bed and
quickly made it over a lump of pillows—prison-movie style,
so that the other body, her former self, lay hunched beneath the covers. That way it did not follow her all day, just
behind her neck where she couldn't see; if she felt it, she

could remember the pillows massed like a snowdrift, and smile away the cold fear.

Jenny propped the framed portrait of Weill and Lenya up on her dresser, informing the house that they were her late parents. Mrs. Hayworth, who always snooped a look on her way to the laundry room, opined that they looked Jewish, but Jenny corrected her: they were Methodists.

The second week of December, the Koval parents came to town and swept Shelley and Keaton up to Vermont for some early skiing. Jenny barely had time to assess these two, whom she'd been privately calling the Missing Links: Nicholas, in his fifties, but very young-looking, with a laughing face and doleful, drooping gray eyes; and Carla, in her thirties, dyed blonde, caustic and careful, with a narrow hawklike nose of which she was clearly proud. For two days the house was a tumult of shouting and hugging and slapping and showing of things. Jenny observed with amazement that Shelley and Keaton laughed at almost anything their father said. There was talk of Jenny's going along to Vermont, but when they learned that the hotel already had facilities for baby-sitting, it was decided that she would stay behind.

Only one conversation took place, when Carla came down to Jenny's room in the evening after the children were asleep. She tapped on the door, and entered.

"They are doing well with you."

"Thank you."

"Maman says you went to college in the U.S.?"

"In Maine."

"And you speak English so well."

"I am vor—working on it." A little laugh.

"It's a shame Isolde is so stupid, otherwise you could

tutor her in languages. How did she ever get into that college?"

"I have no talent for teaching, I think."

"Oh, I don't know. . . . You've been such a help to Shelley—who really is quite smart, as we know. She'd just never adjusted to school. But she's calmer now." Carla hooked a wing of hair back over an ear, revealing a disc of silver and gold on her lobe. "So, you do have talent."

"Thank you."

"What are your plans?" She sat down on the bed, and leaned forward in a confidential manner. "Will you stay awhile? Are Maman and Papa paying you enough? You like the room?" Her blonde football helmet of hair shifted up half an inch along her forehead.

"Well, I am saving for more school."

"Wonderful, good. And Keatsy, well, he's that age, but I'm certain he's no problem."

"He's a little lively," lied Jenny. "But we have fun."

"I think he must be getting the flu, do you know? He's practically down to a crawl. . . . Maybe we shouldn't risk taking him."

"Oh no, he'd be just miserable if you left him behind," said Jenny.

"I'm sure you must think I'm a terrible mother."

"Not at all. I think you're the best kind of mother. You do your own work, and so when you're with them, you're all there." Jenny's eyes opened very large. "It's the German theory behind the kindergarten."

"Really. Yes." She got up, smiling. "Oh, I told Hayworth to let you go through a box of things before they go to the Goodwill. If you see anything—well, it's yours. God knows it won't fit Hayworth."

"Thank you so much."

‖ PIRATE JENNY ‖

"And dear—I think I'm going to bring Shelley with me for a new cut. The braids you've done, all looped up like that, are very charming, really quite *haute,* but I don't think it's what the other little girls are doing now."

"Of course. It was just an idea. I thought they suited her."

"Of course."

The house settled into a hush when they all left. Mrs. Hayworth did her best to keep Jenny away from Mr. Kovalenko, whom she adored, and Mrs. Kovalenko, with whom she feuded. It did not work.

Instead, Jenny found herself often in the second-floor gallery, leaning on the paper-strewn desk and listening to Netta talk about the past, wondering as she did so how much was true. It seemed that when still a young girl, Netta had fallen in love with Nikolai Nikolaievich Kovalenko, though he was a proud boy from a proud family and not much interested in her. Nevertheless, when the Bolsheviks seized power, she persuaded Nikki to leave Russia with her. They stole the family jewels (on both sides) and fled from Moscow to Odessa on the Black Sea, whence they departed, concealed beneath nets in the bottom of a fishing trawler. By the time they reached New York, three boats and four months later, they had been married by the captain of a Finnish passenger liner.

Word of the thefts had reached the relatives in Paris and Chicago, so they stayed put in New York, and Antoinette went to work in a porcelain factory in New Jersey, painting gold rims on teacups and saucers for seven dollars a week. Nikolai Nikolaievich began by selling their jewelry through a shop; eventually he became a partner; and even more eventually he bought out the business. His hatred for work was matched only by his hatred for Jews; nevertheless it was by hard work in a Jew business that he made his fortune in the 1920s, and even held onto it in the 1930s. Whispered rumors of foreign—Italian? German?—investments did not disturb him. It was in the depths of the Depression that he bought the house on 73rd Street.

Meanwhile, the families forgave them, as all successes are forgiven, and a few pieces of the original jewelry (or something very like them) were returned to the Kovalenko dukes and counts now headquartered in Milan. Up into the 1960s, old Nikolai Nikolaievich continued to travel for his gem business, going to South America at least four times a year on extended trips. "Now he is too old and too blind to see the stones, he must sit at home and make me crazy." Netta snapped her lower jaw up and fingered the gold drop bobbing from her left ear. Apparently that was the end of her preposterous tale.

"And the paintings?"

Netta picked herself up from the desk and, carrying her ebony cane beside her like a spear, grabbed Jenny's elbow. The heavy perfume and talcum rose into Jenny's nose, making it twitch like a rabbit's. This was Jenny's first guided tour. Most of the pictures were lit by their own little brass lamps, so isolated pools of light shone on women bathing in a river; on a table stacked with meats and fruits; on a Pan playing his flute; on cows coming home in the rain. They stopped in front of one picture, and the old woman said,

"That, that is my Leonardo." A very dark blue Madonna, baby in her lap, looked demurely out from the canvas in the direction of their feet.

Dominating the main wall was a medieval altarpiece of some eight painted panels, about five feet high, each with a gilt doorframe for its saint. Jenny thought it was dark and nasty, but she could see that Netta was very proud. "Benno found that for me in a little museum outside Florence that went broke in 1938; we saved it, since the place was burned down in the war. It's the only complete one in existence by the Umbrian Master. My son says not, but he thinks he's so smart. Why does the Met come creeping around with invitations and board memberships? Why does the Louvre telephone me on my birthday? They want my altar. Ask me what I paid for it."

"What did you pay for it?"

"Twenty-four hundred dollars. That's it. You can check in my notebooks, maybe someday I'll show you my diaries. All the dates, the places, the prices . . ."

Netta then pointed up to a corner of the ceiling at a ragged shape, like a piece of enormous eggshell. It was some mysteriously mounted painted plaster from the interior of a dome, on which pale pink and blue figures, bolstered by clouds, seemed to be trying to back away from the viewer. "Tiepolo," she snapped, as if expecting an argument.

Jenny examined a murky little pastoral painting, and read the typed label that was stuck to the wall beside it. "What does 'school of' mean?"

"It means my son changed the label to curry favor with his museum friends. Scholars. You have to know the soul to know painting. My son has no soul at all." To Jenny's extreme delight, Netta placed the back of her hand against her forehead and rolled her large, puffy eyes. "Look at the girls he married. The drug addict leaves the baby Isolde to us and runs away in a caravan. Now Carla, the international art thief!" Jenny said nothing. "She works as a dealer, of course, but how could she be so busy and so secretive unless she's stealing? They will be caught. Carla has no real admiration for my paintings, you know. She wants to get her hands on them and *sell* them." She glared at Jenny. "Which one do you like the best?"

"The cows."

"Yes. The German. Wait, I will show you a better one."

She led Jenny to the elevator, and they ascended to the third floor. Jenny was only familiar with the children's rooms, but they passed these and opened the door to Netta's bedroom. The high, wide white-clothed bed had a headboard carved like the desk in the gallery—rosy brown, with strong geometric shapes interrupted periodically by floral festoons. The light was filtered through gauze curtains, but still the silver hair things and makeup things on top of the dressers shone. There was a strong scent of talcum and peppermint, and a heavy white rug. Jenny strangled a sneeze. Netta led her to one of the dressers, and they stared at the painting which hung above it.

It was a landscape, about two and a half by two feet, depicting all four seasons at once. The sky was winter, filled with snowflakes that gathered on the upper, bare branches of the trees. Moving down the painting, on the right, pale buds showed on the twigs, and from a bird's nest, bald baby heads peeped. At the base of the tree, young lovers embraced in the yellow-green grass. Across the bottom sprawled the tableau of summer: a pond with blooming lily pads, a frog, and a mother laughing as her young, sturdy son caught a fish, flinging it into the air with a net. On the left, an old man chopped at an enormous oak tree whose leaves were golden-orange, but turning browner farther up the tree, where a squirrel perched with his nut. The old man looked anxiously up at the snow that dusted the topmost branches.

In the very center, untouched by the seasons, a mountainous horizon was blue and smoky gray. Above the rim, side by side, sat the sun and the crescent moon.

Jenny felt something inside her lurch. Something about the way things went round and round and there was no stopping any of it. Fate, she thought, and it seemed as if she had never known the word before. Then: Who are you, Jenny, to fool around with Fate? Netta's voice interrupted her.

"It's Romantic. Someone named Auermann, but no one's ever heard of him." Netta leaned heavily against her bed. "Have lunch with me." She moved toward the door, braying: "Mau-reen!"

"Shall I run down and give her a message?" asked Jenny.

"Tell her to wake Mr. Kovalenko, and bring us lunch for three."

In her kitchen, Mrs. Hayworth received the news suspiciously. "For three?"

"Yes; that's what she said."

Mrs. Hayworth thumped heavily toward the elevator.

As always, lunch was composed of heated dishes of leftover food from dinner the night before, and, as sometimes, of dinner the night before that as well. Mrs. Hayworth served with a vengeance. Nikki ignored Jenny, and made a good amount of noise with his soup. She was afraid to look at his face, but she watched his small, sturdy hands as he picked unhappily at the leftover casserole on his plate. Netta remarked that the weather was turning cold, but there had been no snow. Jenny said she hoped there was snow in Vermont. Nikki called in a high, feeble voice for Maureen. When Mrs. Hayworth cleared his plate and promised to make him an omelette instead,

Netta muttered, audibly, "Peasant." Jenny kept her eyes lowered.

JENNY'S BIGGEST FEAR WHILE THE CHILDREN WERE AWAY WAS that she would be expected to do more household chores. But she found that by spending the morning talking to Netta, and surreptitiously leaving the house after lunch, she managed to avoid work of any kind. She had learned enough about the relationship between Netta and Mrs. Hayworth to doubt that the latter's complaints to the former would have much effect.

Often, she went to Central Park. But after the pleasure of being among trees (which surprised her; she had never been particularly fond of trees) passed, the park increasingly seemed an uncomfortable mess of grand lanes and squalid byways, of dog shit, radios, and murderous cyclists. But Jenny loved the bridle path and its occasional rider. She'd stand hidden in the bushes near the stone bridge, slithering her feet in the yellow leaves, and wait for hoofbeats. If a horse went by at a gallop, the earth shook fore and aft, there was a long brown flash of light, the rider just barely bent forward, his face, like the horse's, straight ahead. Jenny studied that look, that bored, high-chin look which seemed to take possession of anyone on a horse. It went with the straight back, the immobility of the torso, and it was beautiful.

Otherwise, Jenny would turn east to Madison and Lexington avenues, where all the glittering windows of the boxy little stores clustered. Shoplifting here was almost impossible, but she did manage to pick up the occasional potpourri pillow or vial of rose oil or postcard photo—she took one that showed Lillian Gish blowing a kiss off a gloved

▐▐▐ P I R A T E   J E N N Y ▐▐▐

hand from the window of a train. In a boutique on 79th Street, she acquired a rhinestone-studded hair comb by deftly picking up two at once and sticking one deep in her full red hair while examining the other, which she disdainfully returned to the basket. One long stroll took her down to Saks, where she spent an hour at the makeup counters, emerging with eyebrows plucked high and a white powdered face and her broad mouth sculpted down to a short dark pout, like someone on a Japanese fan.

Chin high, back straight, she endured the startled looks all the way home, then ran into her bathroom in the basement and attacked her face with Vaseline. Though the colors lifted off, her eyebrows remained alarming. Jenny decided she liked them that way, and thereafter kept them pruned, two miniature A-frames of mock surprise. Touchups on her red hair were a matter of trial and error; one color gave her head a violet sheen, like a horsehair sofa.

Jenny's creed, reinforced by Netta, involved shoes—how they said you were right, or, alternatively, how they gave you away if you were wrong. The green suede shoes were right, but they did not work for everyday. She wore a pair of Carla's cast-off lizard flats, barely scuffed, instead. Her nail-biting had recently escalated into chewing the cuticles to a bloody fringe, so she spent a lot of time with some brown silk thread and a needle, repairing Netta's delicate black leather gloves. The linings were grey silk. With extremities well shod, she felt she could go anywhere. Late morning at the big department stores looked ideal for shoplifting.

Wearing the camel's-hair coat that also would have gone to Goodwill if it hadn't gone to her, armed with small sheets of aluminum foil, she was able to head into a store and emerge with at least one thing: a shirt, or a hat—bunched under the coat, its plastic tag firmly wrapped in foil so as not to set off the detectors. But in Bonwit's, a guard saw her snitch a scarf and before she could finger the foil over the tag under her coat like Napoleon, he appeared at her side, took the scarf, and told her that he would see her to the door. She acknowledged his recommendation that she shop elsewhere.

The items that tempted her most were locked onto the racks with bicycle chains, and required the attention and assistance of a clerk. Feeling thwarted but by no means hopeless, Jenny took to studying the stores, wandering past these racks of leather coats, fur coats, leather pants; past elaborately draped cases of jewelry and handbags; wandering through huge floors of women fanning the edges of skirts out of the racks and shaking their heads; through mirrored salons where teenage girls her own age tried on fur coats while an assistant cooed appreciatively and answered questions about the stitching of the skins.

She sewed aluminum foil into the lining of her coat pockets, which made it easier to steal the occasional headband or junk-jewelry trinket, but she was almost distracted, studying those furs and leathers. She finally figured out how she could take this one coat she coveted, a collarless straight grey suede number with onyx buttons. First she would engage the attention of the saleswoman and try the coat on. Then the saleswoman would be distracted by another customer. Jenny would shove her camel coat into a rack and tuck the dingy wool scarf she'd come equipped with into the sleeve of the grey suede. As a second saleswoman came to her aid, she would point to a different coat, try it on, ponder it, and then hand it back. She would put the gray suede back on, and hope that the second saleswoman assumed it was hers. But it was all a long shot, and clearly would require a collaborator. Would Peter help? He

⫼ PIRATE JENNY ⫼

might not approve. In any case, Jenny felt these operations would best be kept solo.

Of course, she thought to herself as she walked up Fifth Avenue back to the house, it would all be so much simpler if she could just steal a credit card. She was sure she could manage a passable forged signature. But, she thought bitterly, she didn't know how to pick pockets; the Dads had promised, but he'd never taught her. Then she shook her head, quickly, so as not to think about him anymore.

ISOLDE ARRIVED FROM CONNECTICUT COLLEGE FOR THE HOLI-day break. Fair-haired, with skin scorched pink from the weather, she barged in the front door one evening in the middle of dinner, with two tall boys in tow.

"Netta! Nikki! I'm home! Are Daddy and Carla back yet? Can you feed my friends some supper? Where's Mrs. Hayworth? Who"—she paused and looked at Jenny, who was quietly chewing on her cubed steak—"is *this?*"

"This is Jenny, dear," said Netta. "She looks after the children."

Jenny swallowed. "How do you do," she said, not moving from her chair.

Isolde narrowed her very blue eyes. "We'll get something to eat in the kitchen." Her nameless attendants silently followed her behind the swinging door.

Christmas officially erupted with the family's return the next day from skiing. Two of the "boys" from Mr. Kovalenko's office, who often ran errands for the old man, hauled in two ten-foot evergreens and planted one in the picture gallery—there to be hung about with all the antique and golden ornaments, and the golden loops and chains. The other tree crowded into the first-floor living room, in front of the glass doors that opened into the garden. Mrs. Hayworth installed the blinking white lights, and then a jumble of old and new ornaments were hung by the family. Nikolai Nikolaievich sat back during the mayhem, drinking his holiday vodka martinis, with a cherry at the bottom and ground black pepper floating on the top. His face was angelic—unwrinkled, pink, babyish—with wavy white hair wisping like clouds from the top of his head. Glasses no longer availed him; he gazed benignly out from milky blue eyes. When Shelley cut her finger on a broken glass ball, and screamed at the blood, Nikolai Nikolaievich laughed, and Jenny saw his many gold teeth.

After the mishap, Isolde marshaled a bandaged Shelley and a subdued Keaton through the assembly of the Christmas Town—hundreds of miniature people, animals, and buildings spread out on carpets of cotton batting that overtook the windowsills, tabletops, mantelpieces, and even areas of the floor. Jenny took a break from tinseling to admire the town, but only Keaton would tell her where the goats went, and the names of the people, and where they got the red wooden horse. Isolde gave Jenny a cold look and said, "It's really a family thing."

Isolde's friends were in the house a lot the week before Christmas. They all seemed, like Isolde, tall, fair, and bony. If they noticed Jenny at all, they did so with stares. Isolde herself never addressed Jenny directly, and referred to her as "the au pair," or "the girl."

Very late, Jenny realized that she would have to find presents for the family. Propelled by Mrs. Hayworth's stories of Orchard Street, Jenny ventured on the subway for the first time. The noise of the trains in the tunnels was appalling; Jenny stared, amazed, at the passengers who kept talking to one another in the howling roar. She spent a day wandering southeast Manhattan, never sure whether she was actually in those places with the resonant names—the Bowery, Chinatown, Little Italy. It hardly felt like the same city; here were so many Asian people, and more black and brown people than Jenny had ever imagined, and shops that let forth delicious food smells, and short stout old people in heavy wool coats who carried enormous plastic shopping bags and smelled like frying. There were junkyard dogs and cats behind the garbage cans, and, even in the cold wind, the smell of urine from every stretch of blank wall. Several grizzled men asked her for money, and she shook her head angrily. It was terrible to think that she could have wound up here instead of at the Addams; it was worse than the one bum who lived in Chester, Joe-Joe, who slept in the Catholic Church and had such a bad smell that on winter days Jenny had dreaded the heat of the church radiator, which wafted the smell up to her pew. She had often annoyed her mother during mass, wrinkling her nose and tugging on Kitten's coat, complaining about the smell and begging to go home. Now she thought: Joe-Joe would look like a classy guy down here. It was the wrong place to shop for the Kovalenkos.

Despite her frozen stare, many men she passed by spoke to her: complimenting her fedora, her skirt, her walk, her lips, her *thing;* recommending she get a tan, different makeup, a good man, *a smile on her face.* She ate a cannoli, she bought a soda from a sidewalk vendor, she shoplifted some pink lace underwear and a black strapless bra. She walked a long time until she found the subway again, but it was the wrong one and she had to ask several people before she finally found the one to 68th Street, East. A young woman with a baby in a stroller asked her for money for a doctor; horrified, and sure that everyone in the car was watching her, Jenny gave her a quarter and was God-blessed.

When she was alone again in her room, her brain rattled in her head, her body rattled in the cement cell, nothing was tied down. This was much worse than that first day, coming down the FDR Drive at dusk, when the city had just stood there like a giant with a hundred big feet for stomping. It was a big wheel, going round and round with no one to stop it, and she was a part of it. She just fit right into the squalor and the fear. That night, when she listened to her cassettes, she was in the streets downtown, walking and singing and snarling in the corners. "Bill's Ballhaus in Bilbao, Bilbao, Bilbao. . . ."

Two days before Christmas, she sneaked into the kitchen late at night and mixed a huge batch of tollhouse cookies, throwing in some rum and applesauce. Although the cookies came out of the oven smelling burned and feeling a trifle squishy, they were intact, so she doused them in confectioner's sugar. Then she packed them in small boxes between sheets of wax paper, tied the boxes up with red and green yarn, and labeled them "Mother's Homestyle German Cookies." Perfect; the right note of care and pathos; Christmas presents from the servant.

Christmas Eve the family stripped the presents. Quantities of new clothing, toys, tickets, trips, and (of course) jewelry were dispensed. The children gave Jenny a wine-red cardigan sweater; Netta and Nikki gave her a tiny gold bar pin with a row of garnets; Carla and Nicholas contributed a membership to the Metropolitan Museum.

"You can go on your day off, and the special lectures are free," Carla said with a big smile.

"She belongs in a museum, if you know what I mean,"

Isolde murmured. Stepmother and stepdaughter glared at each other.

"What a thoughtful present," said Jenny. "I'm sure I'll go all the time."

Isolde was in a relatively balmy mood, and was especially pleased by the present of a week at a spa in Colorado, for two. She repeatedly calculated whom she'd take with her. "Sandra would be fun, but then Katy would find out, and Blair is much too fat, so she'd think it was a *comment* or something. . . . Maybe I'll take David." She looked about quickly but no one was listening. "Just *kid*ding, Daddy!"

Mrs. Hayworth brought out the hot rum punch, and everybody nibbled on Jenny's pitiful cookies. Jenny drank several petite cups of punch very quickly and found herself sliding her eyes flirtatiously at Nicholas.

"Well, another year, another Christmas," said Nicholas. Jenny laughed. He said, "Eat, drink, and be merry, and count me in!" She laughed. He stood up and charged the stereo, and pulled out a worn album. "Jingle Bell Rock!" he shouted, then set the needle on the disc and turned the volume knob up. He began hopping about in the middle of the room, not quite doing the twist—it was more like the movement bodies make on twister-exercise boards.

"Jingle bell, jingle bell, jingle bell *rock,*" he sang, "Ya da da da da *da!* Jingle bell, jingle bell, jingle bell *rock . . .*" Jenny squeaked, stood up, and started to twist with him. "Ya da da da da—"

Carla turned down the volume and said, sweetly, "Merry Christmas, darling," then kissed Nicholas directly on the mouth, for a few long seconds.

"It's after midnight," said Netta. "Joyeux Noel. Bed for the children. Off!"

"Come on, kids," said Jenny. "Bed."

Isolde looked cross. "Certainly not for me. Netta, tell us about Christmas in the old days."

Netta paused and surveyed the room. Jenny and the children stopped in the door. Everyone looked at Netta.

"When Nicholas was just a little boy, we had Christmas one year when the great Chaliapin was staying with us—it was during his great concert tour. He was lonely for his family, so we made a real Russian Christmas. All the people then were so elegant, laughing, parties all the time. We cut snowflakes out of white silk, starched them, and hung them all about the house, and the little babies from the ballet school came and danced in tutus down the big staircase. And little Nicholas said, 'Look at the fairies, look at the fairies!'

"And Nikki's partner, Manny Greenberg, a Jew of course but never mind, big and fat in the Father Christmas suit, and all Nicholas's little friends got real sugarplums, I had the bakery make them specially. Then Chaliapin put on the stocking cap and cried and looked like a sad little elf, so we played—*I* played, for the great Chaliapin!—the piano, and we sang carols and the duet from *Faust.* And my cousins from Chicago sent up a bucket—a big tin bucket, packed in ice—of Lake Michigan caviar, and all the guests, oh the fine people of the town, we all drank champagne and toasted to our health. And all the babies from the ballet and Nicholas's friends fell asleep, tipsy, on the stairs and under the table in the dining room. So there was nothing to do but keep drinking until the sun rose and it was Christmas Day." Netta sighed.

Nikki shook his head. "I don't remember that," he said distinctly. "Not Chaliapin."

Carla turned to Jenny and the children in the doorway. "Night night," she said.

III P I R A T E   J E N N Y III

8

ON CHRISTMAS DAY, AROUND NOON, the doorbell rang its first few notes of "Oranges and Lemons." It was a young couple, friends of Carla's, carrying a big picnic basket lined with a chintz baby quilt, wherein nested a Samoyed puppy.

It was a white ball with points of nose, ears, and tail sticking out, an active pink tongue, and black beads for eyes. Released from the basket, it wiggled over Shelley's shoulder, fell onto the bench, then scuttled through the dining room into the living room, where it peed on a pile of discarded wrapping paper. Running, fussing, and shouting greeted this action, and the puppy furrowed his white brow with concern and backed into the tree—whereupon he wheeled about and began barking at it, with high chirps. A dog, thought Jenny, means trouble.

"What shall we name him?" squealed Carla, as she grabbed him by the middle and held him up in a cuddlesome two-shot.

"White Fang," suggested Shelley.

"Too mean!" said Carla. "He needs somfing sweet and *hand*some, like he's going to be when he's a gweat big doggie!"

"Arthur," said Keaton, which was the name of his best friend at school.

"We already have an Arthur," said Jenny, and succeeded in prying the puppy away from Carla. She took a tiny fold of skin on his belly and pinched it, and he struggled and yelped. She put him down on the floor. He ran under the Christmas tree and sulked.

"My mother," said Jenny, and paused for sentimental reasons. "My mother always said I must smell like a cat, because dogs never liked me. I love them," she added, sadly. Then she sneezed, twice. "Or maybe they are allergic to me, as I am allergic to them."

"Allergies are all in your mind," said Nicholas, as he walked in from the kitchen with a wad of coffee cake in his hand. "You should see a hypnotist."

The elevator door opened, and Netta stepped out. Keaton ran up to her, shouting, "Netta, Netta, we have a puppy but Jenny is sick in her mind."

"An allergy," said Jenny, waving a tissue and smiling. "Nothing serious."

Netta looked at the white ball now jumping at her legs. "Who will walk him?" she demanded. "Who will train him?" Jenny blew her nose, hard.

That evening, Nicholas and Carla sat down with Shelley

⦀ PIRATE JENNY ⦀

and filled out the puppy's AKC papers. By other than democratic means, the name Count Vronsky had been chosen for him. Shelley made a list in a notebook of the vet's name and number, when Vronsky would be taken in for shots, and what dog trainers she should call. Keaton, meanwhile, played intensely with the puppy, singing the theme song from his favorite cartoon.

"Are you having fun with Vronsky?" asked his mother.

"His name is da da da—Spiderman!" Which, thereafter, despite the papers, it was.

The next day, after an ominous throat-clearing, Mrs. Hayworth delivered the message that Jenny had been summoned to the study on the third floor. As Jenny paused in the doorway, Nikolai Nikolaievich switched off the television news.

"Sit down," he said. She did, on the ottoman near his chair. It was the first time he had spoken to her directly. "Read me the newspaper."

She picked up the day's *Times* and started in on the front page. In the middle of a story about Japan's holdings in South Africa, the old man interrupted.

"Your hair is red? In the bright light, it looks red."

"Yes, sir, it's red."

"I like red hair. Keep reading."

The girl's voice was low, clicking on the consonants, so that it reminded him of a slow toy train.

"The dissidents, most of them members of the Socialist Party, have brought a resolution to ban further trade with the South African regime before the diet, or Japanese parliament."

"Socialists!"

"Should I go on?"

"Read something about the parties, the society pages."

Jenny turned through the newspaper slowly, scanning each page. He could see the dark patch of red moving side to side, like a dark, swaying lantern.

"Your hair is the color of garnets. Good thing, to match your new pin."

"Yes, thank you. The pin is very lovely."

"Bric-a-brac. Smart girl like you should know the difference."

"Maybe you could teach me."

"Maybe. Are you going to read?"

Jenny's low voice picked its way through the society pages, stumbling on some of the names, which Nikolai pronounced correctly for her, sometimes. As he sat there, in the murky light, he listened carefully to her voice. "You've gotten your w's under control."

"Yes." Jenny looked pleased. "You noticed."

"I always pay attention to details. It sounded like Stalag 18 when you first came in the door. You do much better now."

"You know," said the girl with obvious care, "I would like to further my studies." Nikolai Nikolaievich was silent.

Jenny kept reading a while longer, into the movie and book reviews.

"That sounds interesting, the book about the bees. You could go buy it at the store and read it to me."

"That's a good idea."

"Do that tomorrow."

"Yes, of course." She left the room without making any noise, and he turned the television back on.

Three evenings passed, during which Jenny read to the old man—first from the newspaper, then from the book about the social structure of the hive. He spoke little but to correct her pronunciation, and she gradually relaxed. Then, on the fourth night, as she read a long entry about the upcoming New Year's Eve galas about town, her voice grew thin with envy and sarcasm, and she put the paper down.

"Kind of like bees, aren't they?" she said. "There's the different hives and each has its queen—and drones and workers. I'm not sure about the royal jelly."

"You think you're pretty smart, don't you? Royal jelly. Maybe you are pretty smart. The word I would employ in this case is—sly. Are you sly, Jenny Freundhopper?"

"It's Freuhoffer."

"Come here."

Jenny stood up and walked to the old man's chair. She seemed to shimmer, red and blue, in the lamplight.

"Kneel down."

She knelt, and the old man ran his hands over her face, not tenderly. "Skin okay," he said. "What have you done with your eyebrows? Oh, here they are. Ugh, I am getting lip goo on my hand." He shook his fingers like a cat shakes a wet paw, then wiped it on the arm of the chair. His hands moved to her shoulders and he could feel the girl shivering. He smiled.

"Oh yes, you should worry. You should *always* worry. But you are smart enough to stay put." His hands ran slowly down her sides and stopped at her waist. "Thin. Very thin. Not really my type, but you never know. Get up."

Jenny stood up suddenly, so that he fell back in his chair. He was breathing irregularly. She stood still.

"You want to go to school?

"Yes, sir."

"What do you want to study?"

Think fast. "Economics."

"Forget it. You'll take some basic business classes. Book-keeping, that sort of thing."

"Yes. Thank you. Where?"

"We'll look into it. Don't push. We are going to help each other out. You're going to be a big help."

"I'll be good."

"Yes, I know. You—you want to be a queen bee yourself someday?" Jenny did not answer. The old man frowned suddenly. "Read to me." She picked up the paper.

The New Year's Eve dinner party was launched like a battleship. The Carlyles, the friends who had brought the puppy, were invited, as was a Mr. Jensen, an art dealer. Over the groans of the rest of the family, Netta invited the third cousins, James and Sally Korsakov, who lived in New Jersey and ran a dry cleaner's. Isolde persuaded her boyfriend, David Potter, to come, explaining loudly that they would probably be leaving right after dinner, there were so many parties.

The children were to be fed early and sent upstairs to watch television until bedtime, since Jenny was to help out with the serving. Around noon on New Year's Eve, as she was going through the silver with Mrs. Hayworth, Netta let out a shriek. "No! It cannot be! Thirteen!"

Nicholas wandered by. "What's the trouble, Mother?"

"Thirteen! With David we'll be thirteen for the New Year!"

"So what, Mother? How silly." He picked up an apple from the dish on the dining-room table and crunched into it.

"Jenny!" called Netta. "Jenny!"

Jenny, who had been listening in the kitchen, popped her head around the door.

▌▌▌ P I R A T E   J E N N Y ▌▌▌

"Jenny dear, I have a special favor to ask you."

"Yes?"

"If you could—after helping Maureen, of course, with everything—if you will join us at dinner?"

"I would like that."

Netta narrowed her froggy eyes. "You have something nice to wear?"

"I'm not sure . . ."

Netta slapped the table with both hands, so that her rings smacked the veneer. "Let's go upstairs. We'll find you something of Carla's—or Isolde's."

They found something, from Carla. Something long and grey and slinky with a scoop neck, and Netta gave Jenny a black net scarf to tie around her shoulders. Netta dismissed the green suede shoes and retrieved a pair of Isolde's old black ballet slippers for the feet. They bunched her hair up in a small knot at the top of her head, with wisps coming down. Netta told her to turn around. "You look like a Paris bohemian. Presentable, I guess. But—what do you do to your hands? Only a stupid girl bites her fingers." Fussing, Netta set her to cold-creaming and scrubbing and soaking and filing and poking at her hands until they looked wrinkled and wan, but tidy. Jenny was too busy all afternoon with her clothes and hands to help in the kitchen after all, so Mrs. Hayworth called her family in Brooklyn and was sent a niece on the subway.

That evening, Jenny came into the living room with her hands behind her back. They were sweating through the cold cream, an unpleasant sensation. The young Hayworth niece, decked out awkwardly in a black dress and white apron, handed Jenny a glass of champagne. Jenny drank it very fast and saw that her hand left a cream smear on the stem. She tried to wipe it off on her dress. Everyone was eating mashed chicken on toast points and listening to Netta tell about New Year's when she was a child. A short, roundish man of about forty years, wearing a dark green suit and a red necktie figured with tiny white reindeer, grabbed her hand.

"Jim Korsakov," he said, and essayed a wink. "A not-so-poor relation." He chuckled at himself.

"That's a wonderful tie," said Jenny, extracting her hand.

"That's nothing!" he exclaimed, and set down his glass. He unbuttoned his jacket. "Matching suspenders!"

A large hand tugged at the jacket. The large hand belonged to a large woman in a black dress with many gold chains around the neck. "Don't, Jim," she said, and removed the cigarette, stained with orange lipstick, from her mouth. She sighed. "You'll frighten her."

Jenny excused herself, and heard the woman's voice behind her saying, "See? I told you." She sidled up behind Nikolai, who, in honor of the occasion, was standing. "Good evening," she said, behind his ear, to make him jump.

"What are *you* doing here?"

"I'm the lucky fourteenth for dinner."

"Lucky you." He turned away, shunning her. Jenny wandered over to where Isolde stood with a very beautiful and very tall young man wearing rimless spectacles. He was in a tuxedo, and muttering to Isolde, "I told you I'd be overdressed." He struggled with his bow tie.

"Not for *later,*" hissed Isolde, and Jenny said, smiling, "Oh, don't take away the tie." He stopped. "One so rarely sees a tuxedo worn well, don't spoil it for the rest of us," she continued, and saw Isolde go a shade whiter.

He half smiled, and stuck out his hand. "Hello, I'm David Potter."

"Jenny Freuhoffer."

"She *works* here," said Isolde loudly, and David looked confused.

Jenny smiled and leaned in close to David, to tell him her delicious secret. "I'm the *girl*," she said, and giggled.

The champagne was still pouring when they sat down at the table, and Jenny's sense of having a good time became strong but undifferentiated. She was under the impression that Mr. Jensen, seated on her left, was captivated by her, though Nicholas, on her right, was very busy with Mrs. Carlyle. Across the table, David, wedged between Isolde (who was not speaking to him) and the Korsakov woman (who spoke to him, frequently, about the food), watched with great dark grey eyes as Jenny said what she assumed were silly, funny things to Mr. Jensen and Mr. Jensen leaned his curly salt-and-pepper head in to laugh.

Suddenly Jenny saw that Netta, seated at the foot of the table, seemed to be sliding down farther and farther on her throne. As her chin was barely above the tablecloth, Jenny plucked on Nicholas's sleeve. "What's happening to your mother?"

"What? Oh." His voice dropped very low. "She's trying to buzz for Maureen. There's an old foot buzzer down there under the carpet—I didn't know the thing was still working."

They watched in delighted horror as Netta sank still farther, till only the top of her powdered yellow hair was visible—and then, inevitably, she just slid to the floor.

"Mother!" Nicholas leaped to his feet.

"Mrs. Kovalenko!"

"Antoinette!"

Netta grimly allowed herself to be hauled up, then bellowed: "Maureen! Get out here! More bread, more creamed onions, more champagne!"

Both Mrs. Hayworth and the niece came running and filled the wineglasses. Several spills occurred.

ⅠⅠⅠ P I R A T E J E N N Y ⅠⅠⅠ

9

CARLA AND NICHOLAS FLED AFTER
Twelfth Night, to their winter house in Seville. Carla was to
curate a special international show in May, "Representa-
tions of Leisure," at the new museum in Cádiz. For a few
days before their exit, she and Nicholas tangled regularly
about the artists she was inviting and the artists she was not
inviting. The household was glad to see them leave.

Snow fell late, but it fell quite without respite in the middle of January, and the enormous city froze still under the
weight of it. A patch of the roof on a house on 72nd Street
was torn away; leaking pipes had flooded the roof, and the
whole section just snapped off one night in a high wind.
Everyone crowded into Mrs. Hayworth's sitting room on

the fourth floor for a good view, but the missing roof re-
vealed only a closet and part of a bathroom, and by the next
morning corrugated metal had been put up to block the
hole.

The curbs along 73rd Street and Madison thickened with
grey, half-frozen liquid that contained chunks of ice and
climbed in over the tops of shoes and boots. The slush
made Keaton cry on his way to school. But Shelley was
entranced, and Jenny was unable to stop her from kneeling
and putting her face close to the grimiest snow patch, or
from licking the ice on the iron railings in front of the
houses.

The last week of January, Jenny began evening classes at
Hunter, in bookkeeping and introductory business administration. Registration was in a yellow-wood gymnasium,
where lines of people laughed and argued and ignored her.
When she finally reached the bald man bent over the forms
and notebooks at the head of the line, she explained sadly
that she was a foreigner with no higher education. After
some confusion and consultation with the other tired men
and women at the long table, the bald man waived the tran-
script requirement and took Mr. Kovalenko's check.

At the bookstore, Jenny selected a notebook with the college logo and a couple of pens. As she stood in the textbook
section, amazed at the prices and trying to figure out how
best to smuggle a couple of them out, she noticed one
young student, his stack of books bound together with a
strap that looked like suspenders, float by. There was
something about his lightness of movement that caught her
attention; she watched, surreptitiously, as he filled his long
arms with numerous books in foreign languages and then
staggered exaggeratedly up to a counter. "Excuse me," he

said, in a nasal, grating tone, "but my professor says we're supposed to read *everything* that Rilke wrote, but you've only got this one and all the rest are in *translation.*"

The large, sullen man behind the counter looked over his glasses and shrugged. The young man's voice got higher: "But you're *supposed* to have these books. Can somebody else help me?" He spilled a few books off his stack as he spoke.

"That's all we got," the counterman said.

"Well," said the young man impatiently, "where's the Balzac?"

"I don't know. You gotta look."

"You do not know where Balzac is? But I need at least four of his novels for my course! Isn't this the *college* book-store?" The young man's voice rose louder and louder. "Don't you need me to buy these books? Don't you know anything about your inventory?"

This was too much for the counterman. "Get outta here," he snarled. "Faggot."

Looking wounded, the young man hurried past the cashier and out of the store, moving again with quick, floating grace, despite the burden of at least fifteen extra books.

Jenny tried this technique, but discovered that the counterman was happy to help her sort out her troubles. She almost got forced into buying an extra volume on computer accounting. What the hell, she shrugged as she handed over three crisp twenties and waited for the couple of ragged ones in change. Nikki was paying anyway.

That night, she showed him the books. He held them in this hands and laughed at the weight. "Going to have to build up your arm muscles," he said. "Think you'll be pretty smart when you've read all this?"

"Maybe. Let's read the paper." She found the society news. "A Clum-ber Spaniel is the favorite to win at West-min-i-ster," she read.

"What's it look like?"

"The photograph is not very good. It's black-and-white, or maybe brown-and-white, with long droopy cheeks. His tail sticks up like a cocktail sausage, and there's kind of feathery fur on it. His name is Saul's Sir Galahad." She looked up. "What kind of a name is that?"

Nikki hacked his little fake cough. "It means his father was a Jew."

MONDAY, THE FIRST NIGHT OF CLASS, THE FLUORESCENT lights and chalk dust gave the room a green glow against the evening blackness. It was exactly like high school, except the students did not talk to each other. Jenny reflected happily on Mrs. Hayworth putting the children to bed and took plenty of notes about labor-management relations. On Thursday night, in a nearly identical classroom, she took a lot of notes about bookkeeping. She smiled at the cute Latino boy who wore a jeans jacket and a blue necktie and who was staring at her.

One Friday morning, as she returned from taking the kids to school, Jenny ran into Mrs. Hayworth, who was walking Spiderman in the ankle-deep slush. The housekeeper stopped her before she could cross the street.

"Jenny! We need you this morning." Spiderman wore a red check coat and a silver choke collar which failed to deter him from pulling. He made a death-rattle noise in the vicinity of Jenny's feet.

"You're choking him," Jenny observed.

"Mrs. K. will tell you all about it—special marketing, a

surprise party for Isolde. She'll be twenty-one tomorrow. Don't you go disappearing on us."

Jenny went into the house. "Netta?" she called, as she took off her coat and boots in the hall. She found the old woman in the kitchen, sitting in front of an enormous recipe book from which newspaper clippings, file cards, and scraps of paper spilled.

"Netta, you need any help?"

"Twenty-one!" said Netta. "So many things to do, and I only just remembered when I looked at the calendar this morning."

"Let's make a list," suggested Jenny, and took up a pen.

"Well—there's her friends to call—if we can get her friend Katy—or is it Sandra—she can do that. And the marketing—oh, how will we ever do it?"

Jenny persuaded Netta to call for the car. Richard, one of Mr. Kovalenko's boys who periodically chauffeured, took them around town. They spent the entire day quite happily at the department store, the butcher's, the chocolatier's, and the fishmonger's. The last stop was at an enormous, odoriferous store downtown, where ropes of herbs and boars' heads and butchered deer hung from the ceiling; where Italian anchovies and Japanese pears and white truffles and tins of purple cookies lined the shelves; where fat white balls of cheese and broad white wheels of oozing cheese and great bricks of yellow cheese jammed the coolers; and where there were still more tins of crackers that smelled of licorice, and bottles of blackberry vinegar and the oils—walnut and avocado and sesame seed and poppy seed—and great slabs of dark red ham and lengths of grey sausage and white sausage and some meat that was covered with a fuzzy green mold and silver-covered chocolates and cherries and baskets of bread.

White-coated youths, smiling the official smile that Jenny understood so well, manned the counters. Netta enlisted one young man and did not let him go until she had spent more than four hundred dollars. She tasted twelve cheeses before she decided on one, she complained of the pancetta but bought a quantity of it anyway, and selected three terrines which came in porcelain dishes surmounted by porcelain heads: a rabbit, a duck, and what Jenny guessed was a grouse. Then Netta ordered two walnut-strawberry-chocolate cakes for the morrow, and, with Jenny trailing behind carrying the bags, sailed from the store.

Richard drove them home in the twilight. They found Mrs. Hayworth polishing the dining-room table. Behind her on the sideboard was her list of designated chores for the party, in Jenny's neat printing.

ABOUT A DOZEN OF ISOLDE'S FRIENDS, THOSE THAT WERE IN town over the weekend, milled about in the living room, nibbling at the terrines and the pickled herring in cream sauce and the thin slices of black bread. Jenny stood behind a table and opened the first bottle of a case of Algerian red wine. As a special gesture, Jenny had tied an enormous pink bow in her hair. The girls eyed it with suspicion.

At the appointed hour, Isolde burst into the house with David. They had been skating. "Jesus, I need a drink," she bellowed, and came through the dining room blowing her nose, her ski cap in her hand and her long fine blond hair flying about her head with static electricity. She stopped short and stared at those assembled. No one said anything.

"Surprise," said Jenny, and giggled.

"Happy birthday," said one of the girls, flatly, and came forward to kiss her.

III PIRATE JENNY III

"You look a real mess," giggled another girl.

"Thanks a *lot*," said Isolde, and blew her nose.

Netta came in from the kitchen, followed by Mrs. Hayworth, who carried both cakes, over which twenty-one candles were distributed. Everyone sang a laconic verse. Isolde blew out the candles and handed the knife to Jenny.

"You cut it," she said, and turned to Netta. "Where's Nikki?"

"He's sleeping. You go up and see him later."

As Isolde attacked her presents, Jenny carefully cut the cake onto the dishes and placed the forks beside them. Only two guests, both boys, took any cake. David came over to get some wine and gazed down at her hair bow.

"You look like a present," he said.

Jenny smiled faintly. "Are you home from college?" she asked.

"No, I graduated last year," he answered sadly. "I'm clerking in a law firm—Dvorak, Carter—have you heard of them?"

"Yes," lied Jenny.

"You should be working there, then," he said. "I never had."

His face had sharp planes all over it, and his eyes behind the glasses were dark grey, with bits of green light in them, like a hawk's. His long fingers seemed to flutter about the stem of his wineglass.

Jenny asked him, gently, "Are you going to be a lawyer, then?"

"I don't know," he said, miserably.

"You should do what you feel like doing," she whispered to him.

He looked directly in her face and blushed. "That's one heck of a bow," he said, before drifting away.

Isolde was exclaiming over a watch when Netta interrupted. "Call your parents."

"Now?"

"Yes."

The phone was duly sought, the call made, and squawks about the thin connection ensued. Isolde was to open the present from Nicholas and Carla, a thick envelope, while on the phone. It contained keys and a note, and Isolde began to scream.

"Oh Daddy, oh great, oh Daddy, oh this is *per*fect"—then turning to her friends, with a broad grin, "It's my own flat! They bought me an apartment!" The tide of squeals and demands for the address swirled around Jenny as she quietly stole away upstairs to the third floor. Nikolai Nikolaievich sat in front of the television. A game show was in progress.

"It's the birthday party," said Jenny.

"So I heard."

"Do you want me to read to you?"

"No. I want you to tell me about your classes."

"There's not much yet. It's boring."

"Boring but important."

"Should I get my notebook?"

"No, sit down here." He pointed to the footstool. She sat. "Anything I need to know about the party?"

"You and Netta gave her a fur hat, with a diamond stickpin. She got an apartment."

"Tell me something I don't know."

Like a machine, Jenny rattled off: "Keats is coming down with a cold. Isolde's friend Katy is having an abortion. Isolde sleeps with her boyfriend and they use condoms. Shelley is not doing very well mentally. Mrs. Hayworth has finished off the single-malt whisky."

Nikolai laughed and stuck his fingers into Jenny's hair and twisted the strands around. "Much better. But what is the problem with Shelley?"

"She's withdrawn and hostile. Maybe it's puberty."

"That's all?"

"I am not sure. Maybe she should see a psychiatrist."

Nikolai turned up the volume on the set, "Tell me what the contestants look like," he said.

"WHERE ARE WE GOING?" SHELLEY DEMANDED. JENNY TUGGED at her arm to keep walking, and they didn't turn off at 79th Street for her school. Jenny had passed a very bad night, filled with nightmares and a vision of her mother, weeping next to a large truck. The truck seemed important, but of course it wasn't, and Jenny hated her dreams. She had overslept and missed breakfast, and now this. Shelley thought Jenny's eyes looked yellow and mean.

"You're going to see a doctor," Jenny said.

"Dr. Warburg doesn't live this way."

"You're seeing a different kind of doctor."

Shelley bit her lower lip. "I'm not sick," she said, softly.

"No, but this is a doctor for your head."

"A *shrink?*" she cried.

"It's just for talking—like—like a very good, very expensive guidance counselor."

Shelley liked her guidance counselor. She smiled and then looked worried again. "It's not about getting my period, is it?"

"Have you gotten your period?"

"No, but we saw the movie at school." Shelley looked up again, nervously. "You're mad at me, aren't you?"

Jenny laughed falsely. "Whatever gave you that idea?"

They found the doctor's building. Jenny sat in the reception room for about an hour. A short, brisk woman came out from behind a door with her hands on Shelley's shoulders. The girl looked cross. "We'll see you next week," the doctor said, and closed her door.

"I'm late for school," said Shelley, when they were back on the street. "Did you call?"

"We took care of it," said Jenny. "How was the visit? Nice?"

"Oh, you know."

"No, I don't know. *I've* never seen a psychiatrist."

Shelley started to cry.

"I'm sorry," said Jenny. "Next time you can go by yourself."

ISOLDE BEGAN TO SPEND MORE TIME IN THE CITY, FIXING UP her new place, which was a few blocks northeast on Park Avenue. Netta's time was taken up with decorator-escorted trips to find furniture and kitchen equipment. The family urged Jenny to move into Isolde's old room, on the fourth floor in the front, but she declined, saying she preferred her cozy nest in the cellar. She was, however, persuaded to accept Isolde's brass bed, which, Netta and Nikki had been astonished to learn, their granddaughter's decorator would not let her keep. The bed was like a giant bird cage of brass, with muntins and curlicues. What Jenny liked best was the way it jingled like a sleigh when she bounced on it.

Right around the same time, some old friends of Isolde's mother called Netta. They had gotten an au pair through an agency, but then the husband had lost custody of his child, and they wouldn't need her anymore. Did Netta know anyone who could use an au pair? The door to the den on the third floor was closed after dinner. The next morning, when Jenny got back from walking the kids to school, Netta brought her into the living room and asked her to sit down.

"We're going to take the MacLeans' au pair," she said. Jenny sat very still. "She's supposed to be a lovely girl, and we hope she'll get along well with the children."

"When do you want me to leave?"

"Oh, good heavens, we don't want you to go!" Netta captured Jenny's hands in hers and jounced them up and down. "You must stay. But we think—maybe—as a sort of assistant."

"Mrs. Hayworth isn't leaving, is she?"

"No, no." Netta laughed. "I am not explaining well at all. We thought—the kinds of special errands—helping me get back to the paintings and all the mail—and eventually helping Nikolai with his books." She whispered, "He's never trusted his accountant, and now we're afraid he may have fallen behind in his taxes."

"Taxes! I don't know . . ."

"Oh no, don't worry about that just yet, that's the reason for your classes. For now, just paperwork, and we'll tell you whatever we need."

"Like a secretary."

"Exactly. A private secretary. We can pay—well, not too much more, but you've got room and board and your classes."

Jenny leaned forward and kissed Netta's dried-apricot cheek. "I would be so happy. It makes us like a family."

Netta looked stern. "You must be around at certain hours, we'll figure everything out on a schedule. I need help when the museum people come, and Mr. Jensen is bringing a load of visitors by next week. It's like a bus tour—but he says whether they come for the paintings or for me, he is not sure." She laughed a little and smoothed her hair.

Jenny asked, "The au pair, where is she from? What country?"

"Oh," said Netta. "You'll be disappointed. She's from England—not a word of another language. But you don't worry. Someday we'll get some Germans for you to chatter away with."

Jenny smiled.

Elizabeth moved in shortly thereafter. She had an accent that she explained was Scouse, a big head with a lot of dark brown hair, a big bosom, and a deep giggle. She loved Keaton and Spiderman and made Shelley and Mrs. Hayworth laugh. Elizabeth planned to go to nanny college back in England, and talked about it all the time. Nikolai Nikolaievich began spending more time downstairs with the children.

David called, two weeks after Isolde moved out. Elizabeth came pounding on her door. "Telephone call for you, Jenny," she bellowed. Jenny went upstairs and took it in the kitchen, where Mrs. Hayworth was banging on the pots in the sink.

"Hello? Who? I can't hear."

"David Potter."

"Oh. Hello."

"I've got this ticket to the theater tomorrow night, and Izzy's up at school. So can you go?"

The next night was introductory business administration. Jenny said she was free.

"Who was that?" asked Mrs. Hayworth.

"An old friend."

Jenny spent the next day in her new routine: going through Netta's mail, sorting the gallery invitations—which the old lady saved, though she rarely went to see any of the shows—and worrying about her clothes. It would have to be the long grey dress; she could wear it over black pants, with a belt, it would look sort of Indian. What did people wear to the theater? Had David said what play they were seeing?

A bit after seven, Jenny put on the gray dress, rolled the skirt up over her pants, and bunched a sweater over that. She put the black purse—the one she'd lifted from a snooty Italian boutique inside Bergdorf Goodman—inside her canvas bag, and hollered, "Off to class!"

Once in the street, she took off the sweater and rolled down the dress. It was cold. She pulled Netta's black cashmere cape and her purse from the bag and stuffed the sweater and the bag into an extra plastic bag, then put that into one of the trash cans. She shuffled the lid gingerly, looking up at the lights in the dining room and in the kitchen, where Mrs. Hayworth stood at the sink. She took the pink bow from her purse and tied it on her head. She moved a couple of doors down and paced. Around seven-thirty, the long limbs of David Cecil Potter unfolded themselves from a taxi and started up the steps.

"David," she half shouted, and ran towards him. "Hi," she breathed. "I was just at the drugstore."

"Hi," he said, and they climbed into the taxi.

"What play are we going to see?"

"*Anna Christie*. It's by Eugene O'Neill, but, uh, I guess you knew that. A revival. You wore the bow."

"I thought you liked it," said Jenny, and smiled her new smile, the soft one.

He reached over and touched the ribbon, then jerked his hand back and they rode to the theater in silence. Forty-fifth Street was lit like a midway, and traffic was stopped dead, so they had to get out of the taxi and walk half a block to the theater. Jenny was frightened by the crowds of people in furs and bright hair, all jamming up to the door. David did not seem to be very sure of himself as an escort; he pushed his glasses up a few times and thought he had lost the tickets, but he hadn't. Inside, women in waitress outfits took the tickets away from David and walked them to their seats, then handed them back with little glossy magazines that were theater programs. It looked like a deluxe movie theater, all done in deep red. Everywhere around them, people greeted acquaintances with shrieks of astonishment, but David stared at his program and did not look up. Jenny wondered if he was ashamed of her.

Soon the lights went out and the curtain rose on a dingy grey house with a rickety staircase that led to a dock. There was mist, and a foghorn. After about twenty minutes Jenny realized miserably that this was the only set; that the lights just moved from one part to another; that only poor people and the poor places they lived would be seen that night on this sumptuous stage framed by plaster flowers and, high, high up in the corners, plaster trumpeters with long gilt horns.

But the slow, agonizing play, performed with a slow, agonizing reverence for life's sufferings, only heightened the excitement Jenny felt sitting next to David. She watched him out of the corner of her eye. He was ridiculously beautiful. People didn't look like this, not really. They would notice from the stage. The actress would forget her lines, and point, and say, "Look. Look at that," and the whole audience would turn to look at this beautiful young man. Jenny named the color of his hair: amber. It was straight, with a little gold in it, cut funny so it spiked on one side, and flopped behind his ears. He wore a tweed jacket which had nearly imperceptible flecks of pink in it, and Jenny almost touched it several times. His necktie was an ugly mustard brown, his shirt white. His legs and feet were too big for the theater seats, and he shifted about. He rolled the program into a telescope, unrolled it, rolled it, getting ink on his long and beautiful hands. Jenny closed her eyes.

"You want to get up?" David used his rolled program as a speaking tube, and Jenny jumped as it struck her ear. "Did you fall asleep? It's intermission."

Jenny frowned and stood up. "No, I was concentrating on how it sounds." She thought of something to say. "O'Neill's language is like *music.*"

Cold glasses of wine awaited in the lobby. They stood around, nervously looking at other people.

"Is there a lot of theater in Germany?"

"Yes. Well, not that much. Cabarets, musicals. *The Threepenny Opera . . .*"

"I saw that once, it was great."

"Where?"

"In Brooklyn, a few years ago. Did you miss it?"

"I was in Maine."

"Oh, right."

In the middle of the last act, David turned and Jenny suddenly smelled him. He smelled like burnt onions and flowers and she thought she was going to faint. She concentrated on the play. Anna Christie was miserable, drunk, falling off her chair. David put his hand on hers. She left it there, shaking, for a minute, then decided what to do: she picked it up and gave it back to his lap.

On the ride back uptown in the taxi, Jenny said nothing while David talked politely of the play, *willing* him to kiss her, to put his hand again on hers. The car stopped on 73rd Street and she got out. He told the driver to wait, and got out too. She turned at the bottom of the steps. He put his hand on the side of her face, and kissed her, hard. She pushed him away, and smiled.

"Good night," he said. And crawled back into the taxi. Jenny waited until it was down the block before opening the trash can and fishing out her things. Nothing, it seemed, was ever really going to be easy.

10

DURING THE RAINY WEEKS OF MARCH,
Jenny became quite attached to one of Netta's umbrellas—
an old-fashioned thing with strong curved black ribs and
salmon-and-black stripes that ran around. The edges were
scalloped high, like a pagoda, and the handle was of clear
plastic, molded in the shape of a feather that curved back
on itself.

One night Jesus, the cute boy in bookkeeping, persuaded
her to go for coffee after class in the cafeteria. She kept
doing things that mesmerized him—like smoking blue fil-
terless French cigarettes, and not inhaling. She was always
fiddling with some complicated assemblage of scarves and
pins and a hat—and there were those flimsy gloves with

three frayed buttons at the wrist, buttons that closed over her blue veins. He watched as she put packet after packet of sugar in her coffee. Jenny enjoyed his helplessness in the face of her accrued feminine details. It was especially gratifying these days; David had not called since the night he'd taken her to the theater, and Netta often mentioned seeing him at Isolde's new place.

She told Jesus that Russians drank tea with a sugar cube wedged behind their teeth. The muscles around his stomach spasmed. He walked her home in the rain, holding her pagoda umbrella so high above her head that she got wet. He saw her eyes, surrounded by soft black haloes, and the water running out of her red mouth.

Shelley's visits to the doctor increased to twice a week. Despite Elizabeth's best nannying, the girl was given to wild outbursts of temper, followed by fits of sobbing. Netta made a halfhearted attempt to talk to the doctor, but she got only the vaguest of insights.

"This woman says Shelley has too many mother figures around her, that she is 'paralyzed by an overabundance of role models.' I wrote it down. She says Shelley should be seeing her three times a week. Does that mean three times as much crying and carrying on? I ask this woman. And she says, 'All change is struggle.' *I* know struggle." She glared at Jenny, who was sitting behind the desk in the gallery.

"You certainly do."

Netta leaned forward on the couch to the low table and dropped a cube of sugar in her tea. "Then I tell the woman about my Aunt Rosa, not on my father's side, the"—her voice dropped to a horrified whisper—"Koropeckyj, U*krain*ian branch of the tree. Aunt Rosa, she was my mother's aunt—my grandmother Sofia and her sister Rosa, they were—peasants." Netta's eyes bugged out. "Milkmaids! . . . Of course, Sofia married the second son of the great family of Mandlikov—but Rosa, though beautiful, was *mad.*" Netta paused, and clucked. "A mad milkmaid. So you see. It runs in the family." She sat and clinked at her teacup with her tiny silver spoon.

"And what did the doctor say?"

Netta shook her head. "Nothing. She said, 'It's interesting.'"

They drank their tea. Jenny turned the carved-ivory letter opener in her hand. The phone rang, and they both jumped. Jenny picked it up.

"Kovalenko residence. . . . This is she."

It was David. Calling from his office. Could she have lunch?

"I'm afraid I'm not free for lunch today."

A drink? Lunch tomorrow?

"Thursday. Before class. Yes—six-thirty. The Rathskeller, Lex and Sixty-sixth? Yes. . . . Don't forget your notebook." She hung up, and smiled at Netta. "Someone from my bookkeeping class."

"A young man?"

"His name is Jesus."

"A spic!"

"He takes good notes." She brought her cup to the low table, and poured herself some more tea. Then she persuaded Netta to drop the desk work for the day. She called the car, and they spent the long, drizzly afternoon sitting on gray velveteen, cruising the still side streets of the Upper East Side, clambering out of the car to see the show of Flemish Old Master drawings at some gallery, to see some eighteenth-century ormolu in a curator's office at the Frick, and for a long teatime at the Mayfair Regent. Whenever Jenny spent time with Netta, she found herself imitating her gestures—which included a half-opened hand, like a claw, waved in an arc above the head; the downward droop at the ends of the mouth; the tilting of the eyes sideways; the fingering of an earring. Netta had given her an old but still presentable mink hat that sat big on Jenny's head, and Netta wore her own silver-fox crown. As they sat on a sofa in the Mayfair lobby, complaining and laughing about the day, they looked to the waiter like parleying chess pieces from opposing sides of the board.

"I THOUGHT YOU WEREN'T COMING."

Jenny shook out her umbrella and sat down in the booth. "Here I am," she said.

"I'm sorry I haven't called." He moved his beer bottle around in circles on the table.

"I'm sure you've been very busy." The waitress appeared. "A Cointreau and soda on ice."

"Let me check, okay?" The waitress disappeared.

"Well, yes," he said. "They've been working me late at the office, you know, grind the galley slaves down—and Izzy's been real busy with her apartment, there's been plants and a housewarming and she's got a cat. . . ."

The waitress came with a tall glass of clear liquid that fizzed in a lethargic way. Jenny drank. "A kitten?" she asked softly.

"No, it's full-grown. A white Persian, someone sells them when they're a year old and not so frisky. It's called Little Izzy," he said quickly. "Actually, just Little."

"That sounds cute," she said, flatly. She thought she'd better leave while she was still angry. "I have a class." She took another swallow, suppressing a gag, and looked at her watch.

||| P I R A T E   J E N N Y |||

"Well, I wanted to say—" He drank.

"Yes?"

"Just, well, I'm confused." He pushed the heels of his hands up to his eyes, and his glasses moved up his forehead. "Aaargh," he said, with a half-laugh. He put his spectacles down on the table and gazed at her myopically with huge, soft eyes. "Help me out here."

Jenny took a deep breath, fumbled in her bag for her cigarettes, and pulled one out, tapping it on the tabletop's thick polyurethane coat. "Help. You. Out," she said, smiling dangerously. She stuck the cigarette in her mouth and, ignoring his fumble for a match, grabbed the pimpled red glass that held a votive candle and shoved it up to her face. "Help you" (she puffed) "out." She noticed that his anorak had toggle buttons.

"Look here, young man. You're confused. But I—I am not confused. *I* do not have a girlfriend with an apartment and a little Persian Izzy. And *I* am not sneaking around in a backstairs manner with the *hired help.*" She inhaled by mistake, and her eyes stung. "*I* have a class in introductory business administration, to which I will now adjourn."

David grabbed her hand and removed her cigarette. He put his head down on her palm and kissed it, on the table. He looked as if he had fallen into his soup. Jenny sat still. Then he lifted his head, took a long drag of her cigarette, exhaled, and grinned at her.

"Have another whatever-you-got and soda. I'll have one, too."

Four hours or so later, they lurched homeward. It had stopped raining, but it was icy, and they fell down in a heap on 69th Street and kept laughing and kissing, so it was several minutes before they stood up. David was sick in a rhododendron down the block on 73rd.

"You stink too much to kiss," she said.

"Can I come in and lie down?"

"Of course not. Go home. Walk. It will help. Go away."
She pushed at his coat, then pulled herself up the stairs.
She let herself in as quietly as possible and made her way
down the basement stairs to her room. There she fell across
the bed, and the sleigh bells tinkled. "Got 'im," she said out
loud. "Bagged 'im, got 'im, nabbed 'im, tracked 'im down
and *shot* 'im." The room waltzed for a while and then
slowed to a walk and she slept.

Jenny woke late the next morning; the sun was flashing
high on the ceiling. There was the sound of a telephone, of
stamping feet, and of someone—Elizabeth?—crying. She
pulled herself out of bed and into the bathroom, drank
several glasses of water, and took a long hot shower. Upstairs the front door slammed. Dressed and made-up, she
crept upstairs to find the house in silence. No one was in the
kitchen. She got herself some coffee and cereal, and sat
down at the dining-room table. She ate slowly. A half hour
later, Elizabeth, Mrs. Hayworth, and Shelley came in the
front door in dead silence. Shelley had a red face that
meant she'd been crying. Fully dressed in hat, overcoat,
and boots, she marched through the dining room to the
elevator. They could hear her crying, loudly, as she ascended.

Mrs. Hayworth and Elizabeth, looking at the ground,
removed their coats and scarves and filed into the kitchen.
Jenny followed.

"Well? What's going on?" No answer. "Is it Netta? Is
Netta all right?"

"Yes," said Elizabeth. "She's back at the school now, in
conference. With Shelley's teacher."

The story was long and obscure in the telling, but Jenny

at last learned that Shelley had been discovered at recess attacking and French-kissing several smaller girls, that she had been invited to leave the school permanently, that the only solution was to send her to Nicholas and Carla in Spain. Suspicion fell, briefly, on Shelley's little girlfriends, on the shrink, and even on poor Elizabeth. But by the time she'd been put on the airplane and the household was having a collective cup of tea on the matter, it was Aunt Rosa who carried all the blame on her late, bony shoulders.

David and Jenny got drunk together three more times before his mother went out of town for Easter and they went to his house instead of a bar. The house was on Sutton Place, both smaller and grander than the Kovalenkos'. As they awkwardly undressed in David's bedroom, Jenny saw that the planes on his chest and back were precise and hard as those on his face, and his skin was the color of copper that wants polishing. She felt as if she were in church, so she turned off the lamp and insisted that he close the curtains to block out the streetlights. He thought she was shy.

MAY DAY WENT UNCELEBRATED IN THE KOVALENKO HOUSE, although Keaton's gym class at school staged a Maypole dance, which Elizabeth and Netta attended. Keaton's spirits had lifted entirely since his sister's departure; he even sang in the house, having lately joined the choir at school. Netta had the baby grand in the living room tuned, and spent a lot of time running Keaton up and down the scales: "Ha ha ha ha ha ha ha. Aspirate, push the air! Ha ha ha ha ha ha ha." Netta found a stack of old sheet music and played, falteringly: "Claire de Lune," the "Water Music," scherzos by Clementi.

The early part of the month was spent in long talks about

the summer; as every year, the household was to relocate to Tupper Lake in the Adirondacks. Nicholas and Carla planned to join them in June, but not Shelley; they'd found a boarding school for her in Pennsylvania, which she was to attend over the summer to catch up. The house was actually on Upper Tupper Lake, and Keaton repeated this over and over as he played with his war robots and with Spiderman. He sang his intervals: "Up-up-up-upper. Tup-tup-tup-tupper."

Netta showed Jenny pictures of the house, a sprawling old white clapboard building with green trim, hedged in by gigantic pine trees, on the edge of a postcard-blue lake.

"We call it the dacha, but it's known up there as a camp," said Netta. "The big hotel at the boat club is just down the shore from our wharf. And, oh, the parties every summer when we were younger! Skiffs would come in at our boat-house with lanterns, Chinese paper lanterns with candles inside, bobbing from them like on gondolas. And there were dance bands, and everyone drinking the local beer. Parties . . . You'll like the club; some very nice fellows work there in the summer, you know, at the bar and on the boats."

David, it appeared, also had fond memories of the dacha. Jenny heard all about it one terrifying night when he took her out to dinner at a fancy restaurant downtown. It was nothing like what she expected a restaurant to be like, not those cozy fancy places in the neighborhood where the Kovalenkos lived. This was more like something from an old movie, which was very difficult when one was in it and not dressed in a long white satin dress with a feather boa and a diamond clip on the wrist. Jenny was once again in the grey scoop-necked dress, with stockings, the black scarf pinned with her garnets and her green suede shoes, but she felt shabby in the company of everyone else in the restaurant. Many women were dressed in black, with tiny black shoes and black bows in their hair. The restaurant was a maze of thick pillars, all lit with pink lamps. There was no carpet on the floor, and the noise was deafening.

A man led them to a table, and pulled out her chair for her. He looks, she thought, like I smell bad. But maybe I'm just imagining things. The tablecloth was heavy, padded almost, beneath her hands, and it draped uncomfortably onto her lap. She put her napkin on top of the tablecloth tail. Of course; that was what you did everywhere. She was a little dismayed by the profusion of cutlery, but Netta sometimes used extra forks, so she felt she could cope. David was no help; he stared at the menu without speaking and frowned when another waiter asked him if they wanted any wine. He let the waiter pick out a wine for him; Jenny thought this was disgraceful.

"Mother knows all about wines," he said apologetically, "but I could never be bothered. Are you going to have a soup?"

Just a soup? Jenny wondered if she could have soup *and* a steak, as in a normal restaurant. "Uh hunh," she said noncommittally.

When the waiter came with the bottle, David smilingly waved at Jenny, so he poured a little blood-red wine in her glass. What did this mean? She drained it quickly. And she smiled.

"I guess it's all right, then," said David, and he and the waiter smirked as he filled their glasses and departed. Jenny instinctively knew she'd done something gauche, but she did not know what. She tried an all-purpose, faintly scornful, "They do not do it that way in Germany," and asked David what he was going to order.

"Gosh," he said. "Salmon?"

Many of the dishes were described in French, or maybe it was Italian, but Jenny saw, triumphantly, a steak with some sort of sauce on the second page. When she ordered it, the waiter wrote nothing down. How can he remember it? she wondered. "How would you like it done?" he asked. "Rare," she replied. *"Bleu?"* What? "Yes," she said, and smiled. "And to start?" he asked. What did he mean? Jenny smiled to buy time.

"Do you want an appetizer?" asked David.

"Ah," said Jenny the foreigner. "Soup, the purée of vegetables." Ha. Got 'em there. Purée.

After she abandoned the effort to eat her raw steak, concentrating instead on scooping the tiny fragments of mushrooms and onions between the tines of her fork, David told her all about the Kovalenkos' house in the Adirondacks, in tones almost as nostalgic as Netta's. He'd been up there a lot last summer, it seemed, and it seemed as well that there were any number of romantic locales: at the boat-club docks, on the many small islands in the middle of the lake, at a rowdy bar in the town. Jenny was sick to death of hearing about it.

"Netta," said Jenny one afternoon when Netta paused while working on the "Moonlight" Sonata, "I'm going to need to enroll for two more classes this summer to keep up my credits. I thought I'd take intermediate business administration and a seminar on arts administration. Doesn't that sound good? If I have time, there's an extra-credit lecture series on corporate taxation, or one on business ethics. Which sounds better?"

Netta banged a chord. "You're coming to Tupper with us."

"Well, that's what I was wondering. Of course, I'd love to

come. But there won't be any real work for me up there, and if you left me to look after the house instead of Mrs. Hayworth, then she could go with you. And of course Elizabeth will look after Keaton. You know I can't cook, and neither can Elizabeth—have you tasted her omelettes?"

A lonely look came over Netta's face.

"Really," said Jenny, "how can I help you both as your assistant if I don't take classes? You could set all sorts of projects for me that I could do while you're gone. Like the correspondence with the Stedelijk about the De Hoogh, and all the cataloguing of the new literature on your painters. And there's the whole library in a mess—not to mention the piles of old correspondence we never get to day to day. You'll be amazed at how everything will be all tidy by September—I promise."

"Won't you be miserable here all alone? New York is terrible in the summer."

"I like being alone. And it's so comfortable here."

"Go talk it over with Nikki."

"Shouldn't I wait until reading time? He's napping now."

"He never naps. He listens to television, and says he's napping so we'll all leave him alone. Go bother him."

The television was on, but Nikolai Nikolaievich was also asleep. Jenny turned off the set. He woke up snuffling like an old dog and blinked angry eyes.

"Is it reading time?"

"No, it's talking time."

He struggled in his chair. "My mouth tastes bad. I need a drink."

Jenny went to the cabinet and poured him a scotch, which he sipped slowly, his long upper lip extended over the rim, trembling.

"Netta says I should talk to you about the summer. We think it would be a good idea if I stayed here and looked after things and took more classes at college."

"I can't see that the classes you've already taken have done much good."

"I need more classes to tell. You won't show me your books, so how do you know about my bookkeeping? I got an A on the final."

"Show it to me."

"They don't give them back."

He sipped. "What's your real motive?"

"What?"

"Why don't you want to go to the mountains?"

"I hate the mountains, and I can't swim."

He laughed and finished the drink. "What a sissy you are. 'I can't swim.' How will you be able to stand being alone in the house with Maureen all summer?"

"She'll go with you. I bet she knows how to swim."

"Like a whale. She came with us when Isolde was younger—that was before anybody thought we needed an au pair. Who's going to read to me?"

"Elizabeth can read to you."

"Hmm. If she knows how. But maybe it won't matter. You're going to find yourself out of a job."

"She won't read what I read," said Jenny, as she slid a thin maroon volume out from behind the books on the third shelf.

Isolde came by for dinner the next week. She was wearing a powder-blue sweater exactly the shade of her contact lenses, and her hair was in a braid that popped out of the top of her head and was tied with a ribbon of the same blue. Elizabeth told her she looked like the cover of *Mademoiselle* magazine, and, scowling, Isolde unbraided the braid. Her look of general outrage became specific when she realized that Jenny was dining with them—Keaton, Elizabeth, and Mrs. Hayworth having all eaten earlier, in the kitchen.

"I didn't know you ate dinner with Nikki and Netta," she said, as rudely as possible. Jenny did not reply.

"Jenny is indispensable," said Netta. "And she reads to Nikki until his dinnertime, so she has to eat with us. Now then, Isolde, which bedroom do you want at the dacha? The front right, with the blue flower curtains?"

"I'm not going to the dacha. Katy and Joe Wilkinson and I have rented a house in Watermill for the summer. I thought Daddy told you."

"But—you had such a lovely time last summer, with all those young men at the club, and your David coming up in August."

"Sorry, Netta. And don't mention David. He's been a major bore lately. I broke up with him."

Jenny chewed her boiled potato very carefully.

"Who is Joe Wilkinson?"

"He's Joseph and Anna Wilkinson's son—remember them from when Daddy was at the museum? Joseph was the lawyer. Anyway, Joe is Katy's boyfriend, sort of. But we're splitting three ways."

Nikki spoke: "So you broke up with your precious David Cecil? I thought you were planning to marry that pansy." He shook his head, lugubriously. "I just hope you kids all know what you're doing, running around with ten boyfriends at once, all these diseases. I hear the news." He banged his fork in his plate. "I just hope you're protected!" he almost shouted.

"Please, please," said Netta. "Maureen! Clear the plates!"

"God, Nikki, lighten up," said Isolde. She got up from

the table and kissed his head, then sauntered into the living room. Nikki leered at Jenny, showing his bottom gold teeth.

When they left at the beginning of June, packed into two cars, with unnecessary lap robes and wicker baskets of food, Jenny felt almost sentimental. They looked so Russian. But then, to step back into the house and close the door! She went to the kitchen and made herself a liverwurst sandwich, and left the mayonnaise jar and the bread out on the table. Chewing on the sandwich, she went up to the gallery on the second floor, sat down at the desk that she now knew to be eighteenth-century English, and put her feet on it. She called David at his office and left a message. She switched off the picture alarm system and ran up to Netta's bedroom. She untwisted the trip wire and took the painting of the four seasons off the wall, brought it back down to the gallery, and propped it against the couch, where she could see it from the desk. It was even more beautiful than she had remembered. She had the ghost of an idea: about how people were trapped in the web of this round and round of time, or fate, and all they do is wiggle the web and pull it tighter. I'm doing my wiggling, she thought. Wasn't there a song about this? But it was abstract; and to think it, to say it, made her feel oddly free. She laughed, one short burst of noise that echoed in the gallery. Then she turned the alarm system back on, took the keys that Netta had given her, and began going through the papers in the desk.

THREE DAYS LATER, AROUND NOON, JENNY WAS WATCHING television in Nikki's study when the doorbell chimed. She ambled very slowly down two flights of stairs, but stopped cold when she saw the front door opening—someone had a key! She grabbed the first heavy thing she saw, a brass bookend.

It was Richard, one of Nikki's boys. He looked as if his face had been carved from a pale, sunbaked piece of wood. Jenny set the bookend down.

"Hi. Did you bring the household money?"

"Hi," he said, adding unnecessarily, "I've got a key." He walked slowly past her and looked into the living room.

"Are you looking for something?"

"Just checking in." He took the stairs, and Jenny followed. He stopped at the second floor and paced along the gallery contemplatively, looking at each painting. Jenny moved behind the desk and stood, watching him. Though he was a young man, his short baseball jacket could not have snapped shut over his already swollen belly. There was a black box at his belt—was it a beeper?

His eyes looked white when he rounded slowly on the desk and gazed past Jenny at the painting of the seasons leaning against the couch. "What's that doing here?"

"I'm writing a new catalogue entry for it." Jenny did her smile. "And I like to look at it."

After touring the rest of the house, Richard returned to the ground floor. Jenny was afraid he would go into her basement, but it did not seem to be on his agenda. He extracted five twenties from his wallet. "I'll be coming by on Tuesdays or Wednesdays," he said. "Now you just give a call down to the office if you need anything." Jenny smiled.

"You got a soda or something?"

"In the fridge," said Jenny.

When he had gulped his last gulp, Richard handed Jenny the aluminum can. She smiled and said, teasingly, "Reporting on me to Nikki, are you?"

"Oh you bet," he said, and let himself out.

11

"YOU DIDN'T TELL ME WHAT TO bring," she said.

"Clothes," replied David, as he stared at the highway. "Play clothes and semi-party clothes. You look fine now."

"I don't have a bathing suit."

"You can wear one of Mother's."

Jenny put on her sunglasses, the narrow green-glass ones she'd found in Netta's dresser. It was also Netta's blue-and-white polka-dot scarf that she had tied, à la Lana Turner, in a hood over her head. Netta had great stuff.

Jenny turned on the radio and looked at the traffic. "I don't like rental cars," she said. "Look at this thing. A beige grandma car." She reached over and ran her hand up David's long thigh.

Impassive as a cat, he picked it up and put it on her lap. "Not while I'm driving," he said.

"Oh please," said Jenny, and lit a joint. Only four for the whole weekend. "What's your mother's maiden name?"

"Originally? Cathcart. Then Potter, Stein, and now— she's working on Murdock. But she goes by CeCe Potter. She likes the sound best, and it matches with me. She's okay, you'll like her. And you'll like Nancy, too. I think." Nancy was David's older sister. She was married to a scientist from India whose name everyone professed to be unable to pronounce, so they just called him Dr. Rudi. Dr. Rudi would not be there this weekend.

"Hey," said Jenny. "You didn't notice."

"What?"

"My nails." She held out her small but pointed fingers, the ends of which were very dark red. "I let them grow, and I got them *done.* Impressive, no?"

"Fingernails continue to grow after death," remarked David.

"I'm looking forward to observing the phenomenon on you," said Jenny.

Cecelia Potter lived on Further Lane in the Long Island town of East Hampton. In summer, the towns along the highway were thick with people—even this early, the last weekend of June. Jenny thought, as they drove down one main street, of a town called Bridgehampton, that there must be some sort of carnival going on. David parked the car.

"Let's have lunch. I told you about this place."

"I thought you said it sold candy."

"No. Ice cream. But it's a real old-fashioned lunch-counter sort of place. We come here all the time."

Tall trees cast a thin, early-summer shade onto the sidewalk. An antiques show had spilled onto the lawn in front of a big white building, where women in straw hats picked up items and gestured with intensity. The Candy Kitchen looked like every dumpy diner and coffee shop Jenny had grown up with. What was the big deal?

"Great!" shouted David. "A booth!" Jenny had never seen him so excited. Big deal. A booth.

The menu was standard. But as Jenny looked around, she saw that the customers were dressed up in fancy beach clothes, though there was no beach in sight. A man with startling white hair, dressed in a lime-green sweater and long plaid shorts, looked disturbingly familiar; she realized that he was the man who owned the furniture chain and advertised his own "warehouse prices" on television. "We care about you *and* your home," she said aloud.

"What?" said David. "I'm going for the burger."

A shout of "Pawww-*ter!*" at the door brought him to his feet. Two guys, one about his size and smoking a cigar, the other about five feet tall, crowded up to the table. They began hitting one another on the backs and arms and saying "Yes" and "Hey hey" and "Summer*time.*"

"When did you get here?" the short guy asked.

"We just got here."

"How long you staying?"

"Just overnight."

"We got in last night," said the cigar, taking it out and knocking the ash on the floor.

"Yeah? How long you staying?"

"We gotta be back to the city on Monday. Hey, we saw Carol."

"Really? When did she get here?"

"She's out here for the month. Changing jobs." Having run out of conversation, the guys shuffled their feet. The taller one said, "So, you at your mom's?"

"Right. There's this thing this afternoon."

"Well, maybe we can call you tomorrow, hit the beach before you leave, hey?"

"Great."

"So, what time you leaving?"

"Maybe four."

"Great. See you."

The guys wandered off to a table in the back. David was grinning. "Great guys," he said. "Wow," he said. "Summer."

Jenny ordered a tuna melt. It was average.

At the register, David agonized for about ten minutes, trying to decide what flavor of ice cream to get, and settled on a half gallon of cinnamon fudge twirl and a half gallon of superfudgy.

As they drove on to East Hampton, the traffic got even heavier. Jenny was already exhausted. But down the side streets nearer the ocean, the crowds thinned. Few houses were actually visible; Jenny presumed that they were lurking behind the fortress walls of fence and shrubbery that lined the road.

The legend on the white gates was CCP. David got out and unlocked them and swung them open. They drove on gravel so fine it was almost sand, and there was the house. Jenny was disappointed; it was no castle, just a two-story gray shingle house with white shutters. But she put on her smile and straightened her long white shorts, tossed a mint in her mouth, and pressed her lipstick together.

"Mother? Mother?"

*"Da*vid. Here we are." The sound came from behind some bushes, where they discovered a cluster of people sitting in the shade of an enormous oak. Tall glasses of thick yellow or pink liquid were distributed about in hands and on tables. A tall, thin woman with nut-brown skin, glaring white teeth, and pure-white straight hair charged forward and grabbed David.

"Darling. *This* must be *Je*nny. *How* lovely." They shook hands, and Jenny beamed.

"We'll just let everybody introduce themselves *as* we go along, and *if* we can remember our own names!" CeCe whooped and handed David her half-empty glass. "Make do with that, dear, there's another batch coming. I *think.*" She lowered her voice and confided, "Helen's been such a problem this year. I think she's in change of life."

She assailed an older, portly gentleman sitting on a chaise, who had a magazine in his lap and a bandanna about his throat. "Ellie, honey, talk to this nice girl *Da*vid's brought to us. Isn't she just perfect? She's an *artist.*"

CeCe pushed Jenny, who sat down on the chaise at the man's feet. Then she took her son with her to the house. He paused at one chair to embrace a younger, dark-haired version of the mother, who Jenny surmised was Nancy.

Jenny smiled at Ellie.

"An artist, dear, are you?" he asked.

Be artistic, Jenny thought. She took a joint out of her bag, lit it, and inhaled. "You bet," she said, and handed it to Ellie, who drew on it heavily. "What time did you get here?" she inquired.

Later that night, the Potter entourage found itself stuffed into an open jeep, which Nancy drove soberly down the yellow line in the middle of the road. A mile or so from the house, she turned the wheel sharply and bounced over a low row of azaleas, then across a long lawn to an enormous angular house from which swing music and loud party sounds emanated. The jeep stopped about two feet from the edge of the bluff, which dropped some twenty feet to the beach.

"Oh my God," said a booming, yet nasal, voice. "I *don't* believe it. CeCe Stein."

Shrieks greeted his news, and the crashers fell out of the jeep and tottered in the direction of what looked like a large and formal gathering. "And the divine Miss Nancy! Gatecrashing!" continued their admirer. "Too wonderful. Come get a drink."

"Is that Davey Potter?" A tall brunette in a low-cut blue dress took David's arm and pulled him into the crowd.

Jenny felt drunk and severely, shockingly wrinkled. Everything had been so much fun, but now she felt and looked like a popped balloon. She was drunk and wrinkled and shabby. It was a nightmare. She would have to change. She walked briskly away from the noise, around to the front of the house. The front door stood open; pushing against the screen, she entered a deserted room. It was palatial, and so ugly that she gasped: a three-floor sort of atrium with white gauze draped over industrial girders, and thick red carpeting along a staircase that zigzagged up the walls. Jenny climbed, fast, and turned into the first bedroom. She looked in the closet—men's clothes; nothing. But maybe the white opera scarf. Who brought an opera scarf to the beach? She took it, and lingered over the cufflinks, but left them.

In the next bedroom, she found what she needed, more or less—an olive sheath. A bit tight, and long. She split one of the seams up the thigh. She looked like an Asian hooker. Tough. She wrapped the white scarf like a cummerbund just under her breasts and grabbed a hair clip off the dresser. In the bathroom, she played with some makeup. Orange lips. Her neck looked very long. The hair she piled artfully messy on top of her head. She was no longer drunk.

She slipped off her sandals and padded downstairs. This time, the aerial view of the room made her laugh. She plucked a white orchid off a plant and fixed it to the clip in her hair. With hobbled gait, she trotted back to the jeep and stuffed her clothes and sandals under a seat. Then she returned to the house by the front door, grabbed a discarded drink, and padded through out onto the terrace. She stood very still and opened her eyes wide until someone talked to her. Then she smiled.

David, who was dancing with the brunette, looked over at her, startled, and she waved. Then Ellie, light of foot, was upon her.

He lifted her fingers to his lips and said, laughing, "Darling, you never looked lovelier." He froze in his bow. An explosion of guffaws behind him indicated that his broad rear end was the source of some amusement. He and Jenny frowned at the two gentlemen in tuxedos who were responsible.

Jenny felt the laughing men eye her. One murmured something, then the other said, in agreement, "Completely deli*cious*." Jenny felt her stomach contract. It had happened. She knew the voice.

She turned away quickly, but Thomas Claverack was quicker. He touched her arm. "Hel-lo again," he said, and did not smile. Jenny moved away and pulled Ellie, protesting, onto the dance floor. Tom watched for a bit, then turned away.

12

DURING THE LONG DRIVE TO NEW Haven, Kitten LaPlante reached over nervously to pat the manila envelope that lay on the seat beside her. It contained papers she had read many times, but still, in the parking lot at a diner, she pinched the metal fasteners and opened the flap, pulled out the onionskin forms with the information typed in, and the yellow memo-pad sheets from the detective's office. He had personalized pads, with a picture of a magnifying glass held up to a face, with the eye seen through the glass three times too big. In a script it said, "From the desk of Charles Coburn, Special Investigations," and his address in Boston. Kitten hated the memo paper. For the last few weeks, she had felt as if she was running a low-grade fever, and the magnified eye kept swelling up in her dreams.

For the first few months after Jenny left, Kitten had hardly dared to do anything, since she was sure the police were watching her. Dan's jeep was recovered, with a fender missing, somewhere in Connecticut, and Kitten had paid for a new fender. For some reason, Dan had not told the police about the missing money from the fridge, so when he told Kitten, she wouldn't replace it. They feuded about it on the telephone for a while, but he finally let it ride.

Kitten insisted to the police that Jenny was not a runaway, that she was visiting friends in Canada whose address she had misplaced. She did not tell them about the fanatic housecleaning that Jenny had done before she left. It was funny, she thought, that the police never even mentioned fingerprints. In any event, they dropped the search after the vehicle was recovered. Markie got a phone call in Delaware from Kitten, because she hoped that was where her daughter had gone. Frank came to visit and they sat up for a night drinking and crying and fell asleep on each other on the couch. He left the next day.

Kitten found the records in Jenny's room, the records with the wild, sad songs. She listened to one side of one record, where a woman with a reedy, trembling voice sang a march, a love song, and another love song, then a kind of talky song punctuated by bitter laughs—all in German. Kitten stuck the records into a bureau drawer with Jenny's old clothes and shut the door. She did not go back in.

She began dating the senior administrator at the nursing home, an older man who was recently widowed. They would go to a movie, then to a restaurant, and he'd complain about the rest of the staff. Or they would rent a movie for Kitten's VCR, and she'd cook dinner. She told him her daughter had moved back to live with her father.

When Markie got his leave at Thanksgiving, he came to Kitten's house, where she was listening to a religious service on the radio and crying. Markie demanded to know where Jenny was, and they had a fight and Kitten kept crying and opened the freezer and showed Markie her turkey dinner in a boil 'n' serve pouch and he stopped yelling and sat down for a drink. Then the nursing home administrator called, and came by, and Kitten introduced Markie as her young brother who was in the Navy. The administrator took them out for dinner at La Cantina, in Hudson, where they ate Mexican Turkey Fiesta with cheddar cheese and bell peppers. The older man told World War II stories and everyone drank chablis.

In January, Kitten called an old boyfriend who lived in Boston, and he found her Charles Coburn. Kitten hated driving to Boston, because the traffic frightened her and she could never find a place to park; but she went, and while she was talking to Chuck, her car got a ticket.

Kitten gave him her only existing photo of Jenny, a candid snap of her bent over laughing, from Markie's high school yearbook. It didn't look much like her. Chuck racked up a lot of hours on the case, keeping Kitten informed in twice-weekly memos, which always included a subtotal of expenses thus far. Although, as he frequently pointed out, the trail was cold, he did find the kids who had stolen the jeep from the mall and threatened them and they told him where it had come from. While living at a nearby motel, he proceeded in a leisurely fashion to query the hundred or so shopkeepers, and came upon the hair salon at last.

Jenny's photo, now decorated with a red lampshade of

hair, was circulated anew, and the trail to New York surmised. When Kitten found out, she tried to tell Chuck to drop the case, but he insisted that his New York network was hot. Kitten was already borrowing money from her friend, and now, as Chuck subcontracted to three New York cronies, the bills became truly alarming.

But they found her. Kitten received a stack of photos that showed her in the street in front of some ritzy house, with that red hair and a load of eye makeup. She stared at the photos and tried to pretend it was someone else, but it wasn't. One thing about Chuck's last memo made no sense: "German alien. No green card."

Kitten worked extra shifts in June, but still had not paid off the whole bill, and still did not know what to do. That Jenny was alive she had never doubted. Never, she repeated to herself, as she knelt in St. Catherine's and tried to pray. So her feelings were not exactly those of relief. She had no one to talk to. She was terrified that if she did not pay Chuck right away he would go to the police. She did not trust Frank. She certainly did not trust Father Laflamme.

In Chester, the Fourth of July involved the dangerous but popular exhibition of fireworks set off from the roof of the Chester Papers mill. The Elks lodge raised money with a raffle—the prize this year was a deluxe paint spray gun, worth about a hundred dollars. Heavy rolls of asbestos matting were laid down on the roof, and the fire department massed about the base of the building in their slickers. As Kitten sat on her front stoop alone and watched the twisting fizzles that went pop and the big blue and red and golden bursts of chrysanthemums, and the bright flashes that went BOOM, she thought about her daughter, and finally got mad.

On Tuesday, July 7, Kitten called in sick to work and got

III PIRATE JENNY III

in her car and drove. In New Haven, she parked the car and boarded the train to New York, still nervously pulling out the papers every half hour or so.

It was after four when the train pulled into Grand Central Station. She was appalled by the crowds. The heat was stupefying, and her pleated skirt lost all its pleats. She asked a news vendor where she could buy a map of the city, but he just shrugged. The bookstore sold her one for five dollars. Clutching the map and the envelope in one hand and her green leather shoulder bag in the other, she hurried past the assorted crummy and sickly souls who seemed to have collapsed in the station lobby from the heat. She found a taxi, got in, then fumbled for her papers and read out the address.

Madison Avenue was stalled out with traffic. The driver cursed and swerved, and Kitten, who had not eaten all day, felt sick. She craned her neck to read the numbered street signs, and felt sicker. At 66th Street, behind another red light, she told the driver to let her out. She paid the fare and tipped him a quarter.

As she weaved up the avenue, her mouth felt parched, so she stopped in a sandwich shop and was charged three dollars for an apple juice, which she drank, furtively, in the street. The map and the envelope were getting stained with sweat from her hand, so she stuffed them into her purse. Her lips were sticky from the juice. At 73rd Street she stopped, uncertain which way to go. She opened the envelope, and the clasp snapped off, and she looked again at the address. She walked toward the trees. The numbers were close. She found the door. That's right, she thought, breathing harder, giddily, it's Connie's house. The iron railing was hot. She climbed the long stairs and pushed the bell. A tune rang inside; she heard a voice shouting, "Richard, is that you?" and then the door opened and a pale face stared into hers. My baby, Kitten thought.

"Connie?"

Jenny looked up into the face of a woman who seemed familiar, standing in a wrinkled, pleading posture, arms half raised toward her. No. No. Jenny lifted a hand that she barely realized was clenched in a fist and punched her mother, hard, in the sternum. Kitten stumbled backwards down two steps and held on to the railing. Jenny shut the door.

Breathing hard, dizzy, she peeked through the glass alongside the door, parting the lacy curtain with one finger. She saw Kitten almost run down the steps, then stop, leaning against the railing. She did not look back at the door, but straightened her skirt and walked back down the block towards Madison, and Jenny saw her turn the corner and keep walking. David, who was sitting in his underwear in front of the air conditioner in the living room, asked who it was, and Jenny said it was the Jehovah's Witnesses. Then she went down into the basement, shaking.

"Remember wise old Solomon," she sang, but her voice was reedy, trembling. She went into the bathroom, stripped, and turned on the cold water in the shower. The water first bit her, then held her numb in its cold mouth as she sobbed.

Late that night, Jenny and David went to a party on a barge tethered in the Hudson River, way downtown. Jenny wore a white silk shift and David ran his palm across her nipples. The river smelled bad, but the lights of the city were yellow and pink and purple and seemed to hum, and everything sort of spun around like stars, though they couldn't see any stars.

The band, called the Lonesome Debonaires, played, and

||| PIRATE JENNY |||

a couple of people set off sparklers and fire rockets left over from the Fourth, and everyone squealed. The band's singer stuck a lit sparkler in his hatband and, crooning into the mike, sang a song that sounded like a love song but was actually about a car. Jenny and David ran into some friends of Isolde's, who gave Jenny fierce looks. Jenny told a funny story about the Jehovah's Witnesses who'd been by her house that day.

13

A POSTCARD CAME FROM NETTA begging Jenny to call. Jenny did. Elizabeth answered the phone, and fetched Netta from "the hammock."

"Jenny, you are never home."

"What do you mean? I'm always home."

"I try every day, morning and afternoon for a week, and you are never at home. Richard says you are not at home and he leaves the money in an envelope."

"Netta, were you dialing the right number? You know you often dial wrong."

"No, I'm sure . . ." Her voice trailed away for a moment. "But dear, this is what I need to know: Did the people from the museum in St. Paul write or telephone?"

"No, Netta."

"Well, if they do, you just set the letter aside for me. And if they call, just tell them I will telephone them in September. It's very private, you understand."

"Of course, Netta. Set the letter aside; tell them you'll call in September. Got it. The cataloguing is going well."

"That's a good girl. Nikki has a summer flu, and we've all been nursing him, but he had to spend a day at the clinic for tests and he is still cross about it. Mad as an old bear! But he is feeling better now. Elizabeth has been reading to him. Children's stories. Keaton is fine, he goes fishing almost every day."

"Netta, was there anything else?"

"No. Yes. Nikki says to study. What?" There were shouts in the background. "Yes, he says to study hard. Call us again, dear. Is everything all right in the house?"

"Everything is perfectly fine. Give my love to Nikki."

"Yes, dear. Goodbye now."

"Goodbye."

Jenny went through the back correspondence with the St. Paul museum, which was tied with a string and stuffed below the false bottom of the top drawer of the desk. In the most guarded of language, the museum had been soliciting the donation of the Kovalenkos' entire collection of paintings and antiquities. Jenny phoned the curator, whose name was Evangeline Spencer.

"Mrs. Spencer," said that lady, after Jenny had made her secretary understand it might be important.

"Yes, hello," said Jenny. "This is Isabella Kovalenko, Antoinette Kovalenko's niece." Good. It was always good to create small confusions. "I've been going through her papers—I'm afraid she's been very unwell lately—and I'm trying to make some sense of her correspondence with you. She asked me to call you."

Mrs. Spencer explained. Negotiations had been in process for nearly five years to get Mrs. Kovalenko's collection into their museum. The sticking point was Mrs. Kovalenko's request that the museum build a new wing to house her things; the museum could not possibly raise the money for the project unless Mrs. Kovalenko publicly committed her collection to them, and Mrs. Kovalenko would not do so until she had the assurance of the wing. So it was, temporarily, a stalemate, but Mrs. Spencer trusted that it would be resolved happily and soon. And that Mrs. Kovalenko would be feeling better shortly, and that her family understood the importance of the museum's commitment to fine art and just how very difficult estate taxes could be.

"I'll do my best to help," said Jenny. "I hope to be talking with you again soon."

Jenny rarely went to class, although she liked the looks of the Tuesday-afternoon lecturer, the one who spoke on business ethics. Jesus, again in her class, said hello, and smiled mournfully at her. In the evenings, Jenny preferred to watch David play tennis at the club where his father had a membership.

She tried to come up with the right animal for him: was he an antelope, or a panther, or a hawk, or what? He moved like all graceful things, so smoothly that there was only movement, careless of his long and delicate, his arboreal limbs, so graceful even in missing and falling to the court. He was like a willow tree, she thought. No, not a tree. Then he would be finished and he would come to sit beside her on the bench, dripping, and she wanted him to stand away from her so she could continue to look at him, she could not bear to touch him because surely her hands would burn away and so she laughed and told him he was disgusting, to go take a shower.

Jenny did not learn to play tennis, but she played at tennis-watching, dreaming up a succession of outfits—long dresses and round sunglasses, hats with flipped brims and white gauze stuff tied around the band. Netta's wardrobe was thoroughly raided, and Jenny spent most of the household money on clothes as well; she was afraid the guards at the department stores were starting to recognize her. She couldn't use a scarf over her hair and the lower part of her face as she had in the winter. David paid for her groceries.

In mid-July, Jenny missed her payment to the garbage-collection company, and the stuff began to putrefy in the cans near the front steps. She and David borrowed a van and trucked it through the tunnel to New Jersey, then dumped it in handfuls over the Palisades. The wind blew up from the Hudson River, and the white, floating bits of trash caught in the limbs of the trees like Christmas decorations. Afterwards Jenny realized she could just call Nikki's office, and then the garbage company. She brought a check over in person and everything was all right.

THOMAS CLAVERACK MADE INQUIRIES, AS HE ALWAYS DID, note by note, like a slow music-box tune. Among the many things about himself that he admired, one was that his mind never raced. It walked, or it danced, slowly, note by note, as in a pavane, and it set the pace for his actions. If he did not accomplish much, what he did, he knew, he did well. How often he pleased himself with the application of vulgar cliché: Not quantity, but quality.

He contrived to get himself invited to one of CeCe Potter's parties on a Saturday night in July. Samuel Murdock, who everyone knew was CeCe's newest target, attended with his daughter. Tom spent the evening chatting up Suzy Murdock. He discovered that she had a long-standing crush on CeCe's son, David, but that David was practically *living* with that horrible Izzy Kovalenko.

"Old news!" shouted Nancy, as she brought the drinks. "David gave the czarina the big booteroo. And, I'm happy to say, he's got a much more interesting specimen on the line. Or he's on hers. Jenny, what's her name. The German painter."

"A painter?" said Tom, and raised his dark eyebrows a centimeter or so. "How thrilling."

"Mother! What's David's Jenny's last name?" shouted Nancy, as she wriggled back into the crowd.

"David's Jenny," said Tom, and smiled. Suzy looked miserable, so he kissed the back of her neck. She quickly left to rejoin her father.

In no big hurry, Tom learned of David's office and David's father's club. Tom played tennis at the club several times with an old friend and then one evening the next court was taken by two very tall young men—and a familiar figure with a red head surmounting a long lilac chiffon dress sat on the bench holding a can of cola. Tom walked slowly towards her and sat down.

"It's so nice to see you again," he said in his deep and pleasant voice.

Jenny tilted her head and half laughed as she extended a limp hand. "I'm not sure . . . do I know you?"

"Oh Jenny," he murmured as he kissed her palm. "Do meet me for coffee tomorrow."

Behind them, on the court, David missed a shot and swore.

"Where?"

"Dolly's. Sixty-fourth between Second and Third. A cute little place. You'll find it charming." He returned to his game.

Tom was not tall, nor particularly slim, and he moved in sudden, jerky motions, completely unlike his speech. Jenny saw, however, that he wanted to win—and that he did.

Later, David asked Jenny, "You know that guy?"

"He's a friend of Netta and Nikki's," she answered.

DOLLY'S WAS A PINK-AND-GREEN-AND-WHITE LUNCHEONETTE, both very old-ladyish and very little-girlish. The brightness made Jenny squint. She put her round sunglasses back on and sat down on the chair with a round green vinyl seat and a curvy wrought-iron back.

"So, you found a chob," he said, and laughed pleasantly at her. He ordered lime rickeys for them both and kept smiling. "I understand you're a painter," he continued.

Jenny frowned. "No, I work as a secretary," she said. "I'm cataloguing paintings."

"Oh," he said. "Nancy's mistake." He twinkled.

"Nancy? Nancy Potter? You know David's sister?"

"Nancy Dasgupta, yes of course, I've known her and her husband for years."

"But you don't know David. He was playing tennis yesterday."

"No, I do not know David." He smiled.

"Well," said Jenny, and folded her straw. "What do you want?"

"Want? Why should I want? Your English has improved considerably, by the way, dear."

"Thank you. I have been studying."

"At Hunter. Yes, I know."

Her face behind the dark glasses was blank. "So you're just being friendly?"

"Of course." He laughed and reached under the table and held her knee. "Friendly."

She shifted her knee away. "What do you do?"

"What do you mean?"

"Do you have a job?"

"A chob? Let's see—no, I am not a lawyer. I do not play the violin. I do not lose other people's money on Wall Street, and I do not wash windows or drive a taxi or teach in a university. No; I do not have a chob."

"Don't you do anything?"

"I do many, many things," he said, and looked serious. "Would you like to do some things with me?"

Jenny did her smile. "Perhaps another time," she said, brightly, and untangled the strap of her purse from the wrought-iron chair back. "I have to get back."

Tom waved for the check, and stood up. "I will walk with you."

"No, no," said Jenny, and waved. "No, I'll just be going," she called, and almost ran out of the shop.

AT NINE A.M. ISOLDE ATE HER MUESLI WITH FEROCIOUS BITES, grinding the almond flakes and dried fruit into a mush before swallowing grimly. Just back from the park, still in her running shorts and T-shirt, she heaved with exercise and with decision. She finished the carton of orange juice and felt like an advertisement. Her very blue eyes glinted back at her from the side of the toaster-oven.

She had left her beach house and returned to the city to *see for herself,* and had scored on the first try. Running along Fifth Avenue, she had seen the two figures coming out of her grandparents' house. Not just side by side; embracing. She bared her teeth at the toaster-oven and went into the living room, where Katy was sleeping on the fold-out couch.

"Get up, get up," Isolde shouted, and whacked at the bare foot sticking up from the sheets. Katy snorted and moaned and sat up, tugging her baby-doll nightie down over her breasts. "What?"

"Get up, we have work to do!"

The round sleepy one strained to open her brown eyes. "Oh, right . . . *Now?*"

"Immediately. Get your ass dressed." Isolde kept talking as she returned to the kitchen. "I *saw* them. This morning. So the house is empty now, and we should get over there."

"Make me some toast."

"Do you know, she was wearing all that makeup in the *morning?* Like a vampire. And God, red lips in the *summer.* I mean, doesn't she *read?*"

"I don't know," demurred Katy, yawning, as she pulled her T-shirt over rumpled shorts and stumbled into the kitchen. "I always thought she looked sort of *artistic*—sort of boho." She chewed on a piece of toast, oblivious to Isolde's outrage. "Really, sort of cute. Of course—she *is* a vampire. No question." She found her glasses on the counter, put them on, and looked almost owlish. "But never underestimate your enemy's strength."

"She's a slut," said Isolde, and slammed Katy's coffee mug on the counter.

The two girls, giggling just a little, opened the door to the house on 73rd Street with Isolde's key. Isolde dashed to the alarm box, where a red light was flashing, and punched in the combination.

"Anyone home?" she bellowed, just to make sure. The house was hushed.

"Will you look at this mess?" demanded Isolde. The kitchen was littered with unwashed dishes and food left out on the counters. Newspapers and piece of clothing were strewn about the dining-room table, and the living room was similarly decorated.

"Oops!" said Katy, picking up a pair of jockey shorts from the floor in front of the couch. "Is this Davey's size?"

Isolde, sifting through papers and clothes, ignored her. "Jesus, this is Netta's! She's ripped it! Who does she think she is?"

Isolde sat down heavily on the couch, picked up a marijuana butt from the ashtray, and lit it. Idly, she played table hockey with an eviscerated condom packet. She did not offer to share the smoke, but Katy, in homage to her friend's distress, overlooked the slight. Isolde took a last drag. "Let's go to her room," she said.

The blinds in the windows were drawn, the air conditioner was on, and the room smelled like refrigerated sex. A black stocking had been tossed over the brass bars of the bed and a teddy lay bunched on a pillow. A pair of men's tennis sneakers was at the foot of the bed.

"Jesus Christ, do they fuck *all the time?*" yelled Isolde, and Katy collapsed in hysterical laughter.

"Oh, Izzy, I'm sorry, it's so awful it's funny. I mean, it's not *funny,* but you should probably just leave it alone, you know?"

But Isolde was grimly shuffling through the dresser drawers. "Where does she get these rags? *More* of Netta's things. I'll give Netta a call, *that's* for sure. . . . Hey, what's this?" She held up a folder with a stack of papers that lay on the bedside table. "Letters! From some museum in Amsterdam! Aha!"

||| PIRATE JENNY |||

Katy peered over her shoulder. "Iz, that's work. She's supposed to be your grandmother's secretary, right? It's the Stedelijk Museum, they're asking her to lend a painting. It's totally cool."

Isolde sat down on the bed and tied the laces of David's sneakers into tiny, hard knots. "I don't know," she muttered sulkily. "She could be part of an international ring of art thieves, planning to steal Netta's paintings."

"Don't get carried away or anything, all right?" said Katy. "Hey! Lotty Lenya!" She pulled the photo from behind a mass of things on top of the dresser.

Isolde looked up. "That's her parents."

"No! She's *Kurt Wale's* daughter? And Lotty Lenya's?" Katy's eyes got rounder behind her glasses.

Isolde frowned. "Her last name is Freuhoffer."

"But this is Lotty Lenya, you know, the singer? And Kurt Wale, he wrote "Mack the Knife"? This is a famous photograph."

"Are you sure?"

"Positive. The New School is rotten with this stuff. Hitler exiles, all that sort of thing. They're *very* famous. These can't be her parents."

"No," said Isolde slowly. "They can't be."

Katy left under protest. Isolde went into the kitchen and put an envelope of popcorn into the microwave, then took it upstairs to her grandfather's den. She turned on the television, sat down, and waited.

Jenny came home around noon. The door slammed behind her as she ran to the alarm box. It was off. "Shit," she said. Then she stopped. She felt sure that she had remembered to turn it on. "Hello? Hello? Is someone home?" She checked quickly through the first floor. The dining room was untouched. No one was about. Slowly, she climbed the staircase, and heard indistinct female voices quarreling. The television; of course.

Isolde was sitting in Nikki's chair, staring at a soap opera. She tossed a popped kernel in her mouth. "Have a seat," she said.

"Hello," said Jenny. "What are you doing here?"

"Just dropped by. Where have *you* been?"

"I thought you had a summer house on Long Island."

"I thought you were looking after this house for my grandparents."

Jenny turned to leave the room. Isolde said, "Just possibly you might be interested to see this," and with a gloating expression, held up the Kurt Weill–Lotte Lenya portrait, liberated from its plastic box.

"What are you doing with that?"

"This? This portrait of Kurt Wale and Lotty Lenny? I thought you said these were your parents."

"They were friends of my parents."

Isolde considered a moment, then shook her head. "No. I remember Netta saying you could tell from the picture that Jenny had her *mother's* eyes and her *father's* mouth."

"You misheard."

"No, no. I can ask her. These are famous people. That can be checked. Besides," she said, turning the glossy page over, "What's *George Gross* doing on the other side? Was he your brother, or what?"

"I don't know who that is," said Jenny, carefully.

"It's *George Gross,* you idiot. Don't you know anything?"

"I know that this maybe isn't very important."

"You mean, Netta and Nikki won't mind that you lied?"

"Maybe not."

"I don't *know,*" said Isolde, and smiled. "But I think so."

"Okay. And then I'll tell them about you."

"What?"

"That you have a cocaine problem. That you're a junkie. You sold all your jewelry to buy drugs and you sleep with old men for money to buy drugs."

Isolde stamped her foot. "Half of that isn't even *true!*"

"Which half?"

"No one has ever paid me to sleep with them!"

"I don't doubt that," said Jenny, and smiled.

"You little shit," said Isolde, and approached her menacingly.

"Who started it?"

"Well, you listen to me. They're my *grand*parents, and they *love* me. So there. So it won't matter what you tell them."

"You sure? Let's try it and see."

"You've been wrecking Netta's clothes."

"No I haven't. You borrowed just as much as me."

"One sweater! I hate her old clothes!"

Jenny smiled and ate some popcorn.

Isolde turned off the television and held up the photograph. "Okay, I won't tell them about your famous non-parents. But on one condition." Jenny got nervous. This sounded bad. It was. "You give me him back."

"No," said Jenny.

"Yes." Isolde looked serious, too. "You dump him and he'll come back to me."

"Why should I? Just to be nice?"

"No. Because I think—I think it's not so much that these aren't your parents, as who really *are*. Am I right?"

"He won't go back to you."

"I'll take care of that. He *loves* me, you know. You're just a—a—*thing.*"

Isolde walked down the stairs, carrying the photo, as Jenny followed behind her.

"Do it real soon," said Isolde, as she stood in the door. She felt very formal, and began to extend her hand for Jenny to shake, but Jenny sneered. Isolde dropped her hand.

JENNY GOT RID OF DAVID QUICKLY, LIKE YANKING A BANDAGE away from a cut. She called him at the office and told him she couldn't see him that night, but made a date with him to come by the following evening. The next day, she went to the business ethics lecture, and smiled at Jesus. She brought him home, and he was still silently admiring the cool dark heaviness of the house when Jenny handed him a condom. They fucked energetically in the living room until the doorbell rang.

"You go get it," she said, and tiptoed behind him as he zipped up his pants. David stood on the steps, holding his office jacket and tie, his sunglasses slipping on his nose, the low sun glinting in his hair. The door opened wide, the three of them looked at each other, and David ran back down the steps. Jesus trailed after Jenny back into the living room and found her gathering up his clothes. He was too upset to ask for a drink of water, so he got dressed and left. He heard the door lock behind him.

Jenny did not call David. He came by early the next morning, bursting in the door with a furious theatricality. His eyes were red and he had not shaved. He began to cry, a strange dry sobbing that sounded like something in a zoo, and then he threw a lamp at the wall, which flashed and made a breaking noise. Jenny did not apologize. In the cool level voice practiced all night, she told him that she was not a one-man woman. She told him that she was tired of him, she told him he was boring in bed, she told him that love never lasts long, and he believed her.

The next week, the photograph of her adopted parents arrived in the mail, with a page of Isolde's baby-blue note paper. "I have a copy," the note said. "Just so you know."

14

JENNY MISSED DAVID, ALL THE TIME.
She missed him losing at tennis, she missed his long arms
and legs sticking into her in bed, she missed how his grey
eyes went black when he wanted her, when he had her. She
opened all the windows and ran the fans for two days to get
his smell out of the house, then she cleaned the refrigerator, oiled all the furniture, dusted. She took Netta's clothes
to the dry cleaner, she called the agency and got a woman
to come and vacuum and do the laundry.

She called Peter at the Addams and he came over for an
evening drink. He was impatient, not ready to laugh; he
must have been miffed that she hadn't called for months.
Jenny mixed a pitcher of martinis and they carried it with

them on a tour of the house. Peter began to thaw. "Oh my dear," he said when he saw a bookcase in Nikki's study, "do you know how much this *cost?*" He said the same thing in Netta's bedroom and in the dining room, all the while rambling on about how they could get a van to come and *clean the place out,* just like that, cart the whole shebang to Sotheby's and then leave for Brazil. It sounded so lame when he said it that Jenny felt ashamed the same idea had occurred to her many times.

They subsided in the living room. Jenny turned the radio up loud and they embarked on a long, drunken squabble about whose ex-boyfriend was better-looking, comparing muscle tone, facial swoon quotient, sexual performance.

"I don't care," Jenny declared. "Mine had it," she thumped her chest, "right here."

"How awkward," said Peter, and giggled uncontrollably. Jenny ignored him. "Maybe," she amended.

She shoved Peter into a taxi at eleven and made herself a new pitcher. She passed out, eventually, on the couch.

Over the next two weeks she thawed the entire contents of the freezer and ate lasagna, waffles, meatballs, blintzes, fish cakes, apple dumplings, beef stew, chicken soup, pea soup, ice cream sandwiches. She got busy at last with the cataloguing, putting all the information about each painting on a file card, with a bibliography. She found a piece of paper with a series of numbers for a lock combination.

Tom Claverack called, twice, but she told him she had the flu. One evening, while she was standing over the sink eating a canned ham, she saw him stroll by, arm in arm with an extraordinary blonde woman, whose hair was piled up and from whose ears cascaded waterfalls of glittering stones.

A few days later, she was sitting in front of the air conditioner at the back of the picture gallery when it occurred to her that she had never been to the museum where, courtesy of Carla and Nicholas, she was a member. The thought of any activity made her hungry, so first she mixed up a couple of bowls of cold cereal with half-and-half and plenty of sugar. She put on her loosest dress and braced herself for the flat smack of wet heat from the street. The household money was running too low for cabs; she walked, slowly, the ten blocks north to the Metropolitan.

The museum was too smooth and too big; she got tired almost immediately. The faces on the Egyptian vases made her think of David. She imagined him, bound in perfumed rags, set into a sarcophagus, with Isolde next to him, while millions of slaves carried blocks on their backs, like ants, to build the pyramid. She stole a picture book of Egyptian vases from the museum gift shop. It was almost too heavy to carry home. At night, numb with gin, she snipped out dozens of little Egyptian men from the book with kitchen shears and hid them around the house. One went into the fern, another among the strings of the piano. One went behind the ketchup in the fridge. (She squeezed some ketchup from the bottle into her mouth.) Around four in the morning, awakened from her sleep by a parched mouth, she feverishly sped about the house removing her little Davids from their hiding places, and then, still in her underwear, she ran down the front steps and dumped them and the book into a garbage can.

She returned to classes at Hunter. She did not let Jesus come home with her again, though she did let him screw her once, standing up, in the park after dark. It seemed to her that she owed him that, but thereafter he turned his face away from her in class, haughtily.

She asked the ethics lecturer out on a date. He said he

‖ PIRATE JENNY ‖

knew this great new place. They went to a club in a half-heartedly converted bus garage on the Lower East Side. He danced like a fool, smiling to himself, gyrating his shoulders and jumping without regard for the beat. She ditched him and went wandering out to the street. Her pink stretch pants had become much too tight; she walked like a cow-puncher.

An enormous limousine was parked near the curb. She crawled in, interrupting a heated embrace between two men. They laughed, and said their names, but she didn't catch them right away. They had heavy accents.

"Jenny," she said, and smiled without moving her hand to shake. She titled her head cutely. "Are you German?"

They laughed some more, and spoke to each other. One looked evil and snarly; the other, very blond one looked sweet, wearing a string tie with a silver heart at the throat. When she asked, they said they knew Peter, sure. They tried to phone him at the Addams but he had left for the evening. "Let's go find him at home," said Jenny. The driver was told to head west, and they meandered in a vague way, with the blond one barking orders from his rosy, angelic mouth. It turned out they meant a different Peter. And no one knew where he lived. So the three spent a long night roaming restaurants and clubs: the blond one, Fritz, would leap from the car and wave to the man at the door and then yank Erik and Jenny (who would be kissing) after him into a dark and bumpy room thick with smoke and music and people pretending not to look at one another. They would stay long enough for Jenny to recognize a song, and then they would leave, as if in a huff, to where the limo was waiting with the motor running. In between stops, Jenny joined them in sniffing a drug which turned out to be heroin and playing with the accessories in the limo. There was a tiny color TV mounted on an accordion bracket. The car pulled over in Chinatown so she could lean out the door and vomit. Fritz gave her a glass of wine to clear her mouth and explained, in a condescendingly simple way, the various merits and demerits of various drugs. Jenny learned a rude German phrase, which she roared out the window at passersby.

A friend of the Germans', a young stockbroker in a hat, joined them outside a club way downtown, Sing-Sing. It was the club's opening night, and a long line of people barked and snapped as Jenny and the Germans and Bart skidded in under the ropes. The club's ceiling was draped in mesh, behind which a flock of live bats trembled intermittently. Sometimes a bat would start to fly, but he could only go twenty feet or so before he'd circle back to the others, squeaking.

"Isn't it *incredible?*" asked Martin, the pasty English boy who owned the place. His dark jacket was flecked white with bat shit. "They're selling tote umbrellas at the bar, but you get one *free,*" he said, as he handed one to the stockbroker.

Bart sneezed. "I think I'm allergic to bats."

"Oh, don't be so *boring,*" said Jenny, and ripped his shirt down the back. He slapped her hand. "Sorry," she said, and giggled, then kissed him. He handed the umbrella to Erik and pulled Fritz into a corner, bought a packet from him, then pulled Jenny back out the door to the limo.

Jenny woke up in a large apartment on the Upper West Side, with some sort of unmelodious diddling, some sort of progressive jazz noise, in her ears. Bart, dressed in a red terry-cloth robe and carrying the Sunday *Times,* approached the bed.

"You look like somebody beat you up," he said.

"Did they?" Her hands touched her face, gingerly.

▌▌▌ P I R A T E J E N N Y ▌▌▌

"Not me." He grinned. "Must be your makeup."

She pulled a sheet around her and lurched to the bathroom, where she was rewarded by the truly awful sight of her own face.

"I'm fixing brunch," said Bart cheerily, as he left the room. "You can read the paper."

Jenny threw up a couple of times and felt much better. She felt a familiar aching in her hip joints and a rawness between her legs. Oh, she thought, vaguely remembering. That's right. Bart. Then she stood under a hot shower and thought about David and cried. She fumbled uncomprehendingly with Bart's electric rotary tooth brush and then gave up and used some old brush that tasted like soap.

She found a clean oxford-cloth shirt and some sweatpants in the dresser. She rolled a bath towel around her hair and intended to fix her makeup, but by the time she found her purse, she couldn't remember why she had been looking for it. With the towel still on her head, she walked into the next room. Bar was busy behind a counter, and the bad odor of eggs emanated from the stove.

"There's a bloody mary on the table," he said. Jenny lunged.

"Can I change the music?" she asked, when she had drained a glass.

"Sure, sure, anything you like."

She walked towards the sound and found a tall black cabinet set into some shelves. Panels of light bounced around in time to the music, and she stubbed her finger a few times before she realized the whole thing was behind a smoky glass door, which she then pried open. She hit a few buttons until the sound went away.

"You've had a shower, I see!" Bart piped. "Did you use the massage attachment?"

"You're very cheerful," Jenny observed.

"I am a morning person. Of course, it's afternoon now." His blondish hair crouched atop his head like a small animal. Otherwise, he was handsome in an ordinary sort of way, with a wide, curling smile.

"Come sit," he said, as he brought two white plates filled with yellow-and-green smell to the table. "Artichoke omelette." He ran back to the counter to get salt and pepper. Jenny sat down, and the towel slid off her head onto the floor.

"Do you want another drink?"

"Sure," said Jenny, and handed him her glass. She stuck a fork into the eggs and the steam rose to her nostrils.

"So," he said, as he brought her the drink. "How do you know Hans und Fritz?"

Who? Oh. Last night. "They are my cousins."

"You're not German."

She swallowed half her drink. "Yes. Educated here. Born there."

"So they're your cousins, hunh? Pretty heavy-duty. But—they can't both be your cousins. If you know what I mean."

"Sure," said Jenny, and chewed her celery. "They're half brothers."

"Half brothers? And? You mean? Pretty kinky," he said, and laughed. "Sorry. Your family."

"There are much kinkier things in my family," said Jenny, and felt the vodka bringing her some voice that was a cross between Lotte Lenya and Netta. "Much kink-i-er. Like me, for instance." She smiled.

"What?" Bart's mouth was full of egg, and it hung partly open as he chewed.

"My father was not really my father. My *grand*father—my mother's father—was my real father."

▓ PIRATE JENNY ▓

"Oh, gee," said Bart, and swallowed. "When did you find out?"

"When my father—who was not my real father—seduced me at the age of thirteen. He told me then. I was quite relieved . . . about him, you see. I disapprove of incest."

Bart nodded solemnly. "It thins the blood."

Jenny said, "My blood is terribly thin. Just look at my arms." She popped the cuff button on her left arm, and pulled the sleeve up. Her veins did look thin, and blue, in her fish-white flesh. "Could I have another wodka," she remarked, and walked into the kitchen.

Bart chewed. "That was just kidding, right? You're very funny." He paused. "Do you think you could get a discount with your cousins? I don't mean to sound mercenary, but their prices are killing me."

Jenny came out of the kitchen carrying a coffee mug brimming with vodka. "I never interfere in the family business," she intoned. She stood behind Bart and put her arms around his neck in a limp headlock. "There's," she whispered, "*mad*ness in the family." She licked his ear.

SO FAR, AUGUST HAD FULFILLED EVERY EXPECTATION; IT WAS hot, it was muggy, it was dirty, everyone was pissed off all the time. Safe in the cool, air-conditioned Kovalenko house, Jenny worked at sorting and cataloguing. After a couple of frustrating weeks, she at last located the lock which the combination fit. It went with a baby-sized safe in Nikki's study, tucked away behind the television set. Inside was a stash of jewelry: heavy, ugly clip earrings set with what looked like topazes; bracelets with diamonds; a couple of dozen stickpins with heads of emeralds and rubies and pearls and gold animals; tiny, threadlike looping gold and

silver chains attached to pins shaped like feathers and this-
tles and daisies; a velvet box containing a long string of
pearls, alternating black and white; several ornate lady's
watches; cufflinks and shirt studs and oddments of uniden-
tifiable use; rings of green and red and yellow and orange
and clear and aqua stones; a necklace of pink stones; some
cameos; and, how amazing, a tiara. Jenny cursed Nikki for
not having fulfilled his promise to teach her how to tell
good jewelry from bad. She did not remove anything, but
gently closed the safe.

That weekend Jenny went as Bart's date up the Hudson
River to the town of Thunderhead. They drove in Bart's
big, comfortable car, a vintage sedan, he told her, but she
had long ago learned that she didn't have to pay attention
when men talked about cars. How quickly the city fell away,
and the green took over along the river, amazed her. They
rolled, smooth and fast, and Jenny dozed in the hot sun.

Dave and Judy Something were their hosts—Jenny
couldn't get the last name, and stopped trying. Dave and
Judy were happily restoring a nineteenth-century house
but, as they explained, they weren't going to be slaves to
accuracy. After all, some changes are good changes. The
bathrooms, for instance, had sunken tubs. The windows
were thermal pane. The stove had a convection oven.

The house, embedded in cute shrubbery and flower beds
and pots of geraniums, sat on a side street just off the
town's main thoroughfare, a broad promenade of tea shops
and antique nooks and whatnot stores sloping gently down
to a gazebo overlooking the water. On weekends, Bart and
his kind strode the streets purposefully, hands thrust into
khaki pockets, jingling change, or else carrying sleek plastic
radios that no longer worked and brightly colored dishes

and old tobacconist's signs and tins of throat lozenges from the 1930s. Jenny got Bart to buy her a stack of antique cotton nighties with lace smocking, and Bart openly preened at the joshing he got from Dave when they unwrapped them on the butcher block in the kitchen.

"Aren't they divine?" said Judy. She pouted elaborately and put Dave's arm around her shoulder. "How come you never get me anything like that?"

"Why should I?" boomed Dave. "We're married!" He and Bart cracked up.

While Dave painted the basement, Judy cooked: "Cold melon soup, veal with gooseberries, asparagus—some kind of sorbet, don't you think? Dave honey? Lime or ginger sorbet?" Bart energetically shaved the hundred square feet of lawn, and Jenny went for a long walk. After shoplifting a straw hat from Remembrance of Things Past, she sat on the patio of the Thunderhead Inn overlooking the river until an old man bought her a drink.

When she got back to Dave and Judy's, the other guests had already arrived. Bart had his videocam out and was enjoining the gathering to act normal. Jenny stuck on her smile and drank bourbon and kept smiling all through dinner and all the Beaujolais, while the conversation whirled to giddy heights of speculation about a new movie (someone knew the director) and the economy and someone's boat and someone's house and someone's bathroom fixtures and several people's cars.

After dinner, they switched on the television and everyone laughed at the music videos and drank cognac and Dave lit a cigar. Jenny smiled and said she had a headache, and retired upstairs.

It was a profound relief to be alone. But her heart was

racing and she felt her body moving away from her. It was probably the drink. She had a flask in her suitcase, and drank some more. "Drinking too much," she admonished herself, and had another swallow. She changed into one of her new long white nightgowns, which was too big. The lace sagged down over her breasts. She yanked it down in the back and, feeling like a ghost, floated barefoot down the stairs and, undetected, out the kitchen door.

The streetlamps were irregularly placed, and she darted down to the river in the shadows of the houses, lurking fearfully when a laughing couple, then a bicycle, passed. She made it down to the gazebo, and as she stood there on the platform watched the swans on the river. Across the wide flat water, at least a mile away, loomed a rocky crag lit crossways by a ribbon of sparkling light as cars climbed the road to the top.

"Oh, moon of Alabama . . ." Her throat was too dry to sing.

She climbed over the gazebo trellis and onto the rocks. The swans bulked towards her. One hissed. She waded out to her neck, her feet hurting vaguely, and then she had to swim. The current was strong, and suddenly she was very, very cold.

She pushed with all her strength against the dark coldness that wanted to take her away. She fought back to shore, against the yanking coldness and the vast silence of the river. It seemed to last forever, but her mind was filled up with blackness: the black sky that was free, and beckoning; and the blacker water, heavy like oil, that sucked her down and turned her flesh to black stone.

She finally banged up on the rocks about a hundred yards down from the swans. Rocks and refuse cut her feet and her knees as she climbed out of the water. She bled soggily through her nightgown, she bled on the lawns as she limped back the way she had come. The lace on the bodice was torn. She sneaked under the windows of the house— the other guests had left, and Judy was clattering around in the kitchen. Bart and Dave were still watching television. She darted through the front door and up the stairs and into the bathroom.

She lay on the floor and stared at the light fixture and thought about escape. It was a prison movie again. And the world went round and round, so where could anyone really go? She noticed that the light fixture was hanging at an angle, with a few wires showing Dave's bad carpentry. Well, there were places that would be better than here. She hauled herself up from the floor and bathed her wounds with a cold facecloth. It was time to think about it.

15

JENNY WALKED QUICKLY UP TO THE
Germans, and grabbed their arms. She winked at Erik's
dark eyes and kissed Fritz's pale cheek.

"Call me Cousin Jenny," she commanded, then turned
with them to smile at Bart, who was wearing a leather bom-
bardier's jacket and a baseball cap. Maybe she could make
this work.

"Cousin Jenny," shrieked Erik obligingly, while Fritz
shook Bart's hand.

"Family reunion," said Bart, and grinned. "Let's get a
drink. I'm buying." They rushed the bar, while Bart whee-
dled a table out of the majordomo at the desk.

During the meal, a translucent ravioli consumed with

chopsticks and accompanied by heavy red wine, Erik, who was very high, elaborated on the family theme and told of childhood romps in the Black Forest, the Rhineland castle where they spent their delightful summers, Cousin Jenny's first day at school and how they had all cried. He was overdoing it. While he talked, Erik slid his hand up Jenny's skirt and tucked his fingers into the top of her stocking.

Bart left to schmooze another table. Jenny refastened her garter and spoke urgently to Fritz. "I have a proposition to make," she said, low.

"We need privacy?"

"Yes."

The two of them sauntered back to the ladies' room. She went in first, and waited while the Japanese woman at the mirror finished inspecting her teeth. After she left, Jenny opened the door, and Fritz stepped in. He braced himself in the door, effectively blocking anyone else's entrance, and in the process smeared the mirror with his hair grease. He looked less angelic in this light, his blue eyes washed light and pinkish skin rubbed raw at the temples.

"I need a passport," said Jenny.

Fritz smiled. "Go to the passport bureau."

"A German passport."

"Well, I think you will have problems."

"I want you to help me."

Fritz looked pained. "How could I do that? What do I know about passports? Do I look like a customs officer?"

"You look like a smart man who can do things."

"You have made a mistake." Fritz turned to open the door, deeply offended. "Next you will call me names."

Jenny put her hand on his on the knob. "Stop this," she said. "I need your help. I keep secrets. I can pay. Look at me."

Fritz looked and saw thin, pale skin stretched over a structure of stainless steel. He smiled. "For you?"

"Yes, for me. How much will it cost?"

"Cost de-pends. I can get you one secondhand, we replace the photograph . . ."

"How much will that cost?"

He shrugged, and licked his lips. "I can get it for maybe five hundred. Maybe."

"And what about a new one, in my own name?"

"Oh, now we are talking ex*pen*sive."

"How much?"

"Thirty, thirty-five hundred. I am not sure. This is not my—my habit. I will see."

"I want both." She yanked a paper towel from the holder and ran it under the tap. "Now, for payment—can I arrange a trade?"

Fritz sighed disgustedly. "Oh, cousin, I don't know—maybe Erik would be interested, but then you must do business with him. . . ."

"No, no." Jenny mopped her forehead and neck. "Not that."

THE KOVALENKO ENTOURAGE RETURNED FROM THE ADIRON-dacks Labor Day weekend, bulging out of their cars, moaning about the traffic. Unpacking and banging about continued for a few hours. Suddenly, screams issued from the basement. Mrs. Hayworth, gone white beneath sun-reddened skin, charged upstairs.

"Mrs. K.! Mrs. K.! Everything's gone!"

Netta leaned over the stairrail on the third floor and screamed back, "Nikki's taking a nap! Keep quiet!" She

III P I R A T E J E N N Y III

tottered down to the ground floor. Mrs. Hayworth was still shouting.

"She's taken it all! All the food! The meatballs, the stews, the blintzes! My freezer has been robbed!"

Netta clasped her hands to her breast and drew in her breath. Her eyes popped. "You are *screaming* about your *freezer?*"

"She ate everything while we were gone!"

"You expect the girl to starve to death? Of course she ate your freezer. That's why the food is there, no? To eat!"

Mrs. Hayworth whimpered. "Everything was planned for the month—what on earth will I do?"

"You will cook."

Jenny found Nikki asleep in his old chair. She poured him a scotch and sat on his footstool until he woke up.

"You," he said, patting her behind as she handed him the drink. "You've filled out some," he leered.

"I was fatter two weeks ago," said Jenny. "You should have seen me then."

"Not interested."

"Shall I read the newspaper?"

"When I was sick, Elizabeth sat on the bed to read me fairy tales. She almost tipped the bed over. When I got better, she sat beside me on the couch."

Jenny sighed. "That's nice," she said.

"Tell me about business classes."

"They are always boring, but I learned something about taxes. You can show me your books anytime."

Nikolai Nikolaievich sipped his drink from shaking hands. "My Jew accountant came to see me in the mountains. He's made a deal with the IRS for me, somehow we pay them off over the next ten years. Maybe a little something for the Jew under the table, but I do not care. No more problems. So I do not think you need to see the books after all."

Jenny had been dismissed. "And no reading?"

"Elizabeth has a lovely voice."

As Jenny went downstairs, the phone rang. She could hear Netta, sounding unnaturally giddy.

"No, just back from the mountains, our camp on the lake. Yes—Tupper Lake. Yes, Nikolai is well, he had the flu—no, not too serious—and the cataracts, but he refuses the surgery. . . . I know—Shelley's in Beechcroft, Pennsylvania, and Keats is still with us—you never met him? A long time. Isolde, yes, Isolde's all grown up now, she has her own place. Just the leg, but I'm very well, thank you, yes, we had the elevator put in over the last summer. Yes? Yes? No. Well. That sounds like—well, you know I'm so terribly busy with the collection here, but—oh, well, a good cause, yes, I know. If you really need me. Just this once. Yes. Let me get me calendar." She put her hand over the mouthpiece. "Jenny?"

"Yes, Netta?"

"Run and get me my calendar. I think it's on the table in the living room. . . . Uh hunh. Married? Again? No, no. She's back and forth with that Potter child. Yes, they came up for the last two weeks. He's very gloomy, I think, like a poet, and Izzy just seems . . . Yes, that's right, she's on your committee? Yes—" Jenny brought her the book. "Here we are. October the fourteenth. Yes. At the gallery. Two P.M. You are welcome. Yes of course. Yes. Goodbye."

Netta hung up the phone, looking as if she'd been asked to the prom. "Well," she said, and she puffed up her chest importantly. "They've invited me to judge the draw-

||| PIRATE JENNY |||

ings at the Saddler Gallery. It's a benefit for the Met's conservancy program. She's chairing the benefit, and she asked *me.*"

"Who is she?" asked Jenny.

Netta looked at her in astonishment. "Constance Claverack," she said. "But of course, how would you know?"

THE NEXT WEEK, WHILE BART WAS AWAY ON A BUSINESS TRIP, Jenny took the afternoon to run errands. But contrary to her announcement, they were not errands for Netta. She went by Bart's building and smiled at the old Polish doorman, who knew her. She came back down the elevator with a bag of laundry in a wheeled wire basket, which she rolled around the corner to the van. A cadaverous old black man helped her unload the cameras, the videocam, the two VCRs, the jewelry, the leather jackets and pants, the vicuña coat. Jenny handed the man a sealed envelope on which the word "Cousin" was written. In it were some small square photos of herself, taken the previous week in a photo booth.

She wheeled the empty cart back into the lobby. "Dropped it off," she said, and laughed. She bummed a cigarette from the doorman and watched a Western with him for five minutes, then brought the cart back upstairs and left.

Fritz called that night.

"Well?" she said.

"It will be tight. I do not know if I can do it. I have the materials. The card will help. When does he get back?"

"Friday."

"Nothing wrong?"

"No."

"I'll call next week. Erik sends a vet, vet kiss."

JENNY CONSOLED BART AND ENCOURAGED HIS BELIEF THAT
the Haitian super was implicated, since he was the only
person who could possibly have a key. After he hung up the
phone on the insurance agent, she told him to cancel his
stolen credit card, which he did, and kissed her gratefully
for reminding him. He then asked her to leave, explaining
that he was just too upset to be intimate right now. Jenny
pouted prettily but was very understanding. On Monday,
she sent flowers (charged to Netta's account) to his office,
and called every day to consult the level of his bereave-
ment. All that week, Fritz failed to call.

Friday, Bart cooked dinner for Jenny in his apartment
and Fritz dropped by with some complimentary drugs. He
stayed long enough to share three bottles of champagne.
When Jenny left Bart asleep in his bed around one, the
passports were in her purse. One was French, in the name
of Karin-Claude Gaumont, who was thirty, with brown hair
and green eyes. The other, the new one, was for Jenny
Freuhoffer, twenty-two, brown hair, hazel eyes, and indicated an extended visa dating from two years previous.
Jenny was annoyed, again, by the photos that gave her a
thick neck.

Every day, several times a day, Jenny would think about
those small square passport books. They were like tickets to
a play, but she did not yet know the date of the performance. Sometimes the thought of them, or the touch of
them, made her feel safe; sometimes the very idea of escape
that they gave her filled her with dread. She went with Elizabeth and Keaton to the children's carousel in the park. She

||| P I R A T E   J E N N Y |||

hadn't been on a merry-go-round since she was a small girl, and she was a little frightened at how fast it went. Her leering pony, with its pale brown billows of mane, seemed to want to throw her; so, as the wheel spun, she climbed off and staggered to a lower mount, a pinkish hippopotamus, and managed to drape herself sidesaddle onto him. She almost fell off again, and sick with the ride, pondered how far away the passports could really take her.

The week before the benefit, Mrs. Claverack and her son, Thomas, came to dinner. Tom gravely inclined his head on meeting Jenny, and disengaged his hand. Other committee members came, and the talk was of museums and children and the ballet. Tom went on cleverly about drawings—it seemed he had a collection—and ignored Jenny. His face was sleek and full, his dark eyes very round and shiny, in the candlelight. He was attentive to his mother, a stern Christian specimen impeccably dressed and coiffed, without a speck of makeup. He also murmured some to the blonde woman seated at his side, whom Jenny guessed to be the one she had seen him with in August, and whose name was Caroline Somebody.

Jenny was too wary to drink, and unable to eat. She dropped her knife in the lap of her neighbor—Dr. Whoever—and though she smiled her best smile, he remained offended. She was dressed in a sweater and a wool skirt, and the room was very hot. She felt the wetness under her arms spread up to her neck, and wondered if she was ill. At one point, observing that Netta was sliding ominously low in her chair, she seized the chance to get up and fetch Mrs. Hayworth. Then she contrived to help out in the kitchen, and did not return to the table.

After coffee, the group went up to the gallery for a tour. Jenny slipped away towards the basement, but someone caught her arm. Tom pushed her in front of him down a few steps and pinned her shoulders with his arms while he shoved his knee between her legs.

"Don't look confused," he purred. "I know you are not confused." And he bit her neck until she shivered, and then he let her go and quickly trotted back up the steps to rejoin the crowd, closing the basement door quietly behind him.

"Nein," whispered Jenny.

TOM SAT WITH HIS MOTHER IN THE RIGHT FRONT PEW, WHERE she could get a good look at the Most Reverend Peter Montayne as he delivered his sermon. He spoke on "Lifting Our Hearts," but when he saw the widow of his former pastor gazing at him with iron eyes, his own heart sank. The sermon entailed long and what had no doubt once struck the poor man as eloquent metaphors: birds soared, buildings rose, helicopters flew, rocket ships blasted off. Mrs. Claverack clutched her son's hand.

"Mother," he said as he walked her home, "you shouldn't look at Peter like that. He goes all jittery."

"Helicopters," she remarked. Her son laughed.

Constance Claverack inhabited one of the last intact houses on Gramercy Park. The entry hall was tall, in the manner of 1870. Dinner would be ready shortly. Tom brought her a sweet vermouth on the rocks, which she drank sparingly, shifting uncomfortably on the loveseat as the topic approached.

"Well?"

"I can't say I'm terribly impressed. She seems very clumsy. And the eyes."

"It's a style, Mother. Bohemian. She was born in Germany, after all. She says."

III   P I R A T E   J E N N Y   III

"Good heavens, Thomas, you must know where she comes from!"

"Does it really matter? Nobody expects this to last forever. Just enough to take the pressure off."

"You haven't been very discreet. You think it's very high church of me, but I believe your late father knows about it. And I'm sure he isn't one bit pleased."

"Mother, that's a grotesque remark. Anyway, surely he forgives me."

"I'm not sure *I* do."

They sat down to creamed chicken, baked potatoes, peas, and sour white wine.

"Anyway," said Tom, as he chewed on a carrot stick, "it's not just for the other reasons. I like her."

"I thought you liked Caroline."

"Different way. Besides, she turned me down."

"No!"

"Yes, she did. I guess she knows."

"That's very narrow of her. We all have our pasts."

"Do you have a past?"

"That's a rude question," she replied. There was a shade of a smile around her mouth.

Tom liked the drawing-room-comedy quality his mother possessed, especially now that all her instincts had been marshaled for this fictional necessity that her son take a wife. One rude remark from a trustee about Thomas's habits, and she was at arms against a sea of foreseen troubles.

Tom sat down with a glass of good wine in his own apartment, some blocks north. Emilio, a slender boy with a long nose and no hips, padded into the room in his stocking feet. He put Ravel's "Mother Goose" on the disc player, then poured himself a glass and lay down on the sofa, putting his head in Tom's lap and staring at the ceiling. Tom ran his index finger up and down Emilio's nose, making him sneeze, high, like a cat.

The East River was bright gray, thick with sailboats and powerboats. An enormous barge lumbered upstream. Tom ran his hand through the boy's coarse black hair and thought about the girl. She had looked so worried, but her eyes were steady. What with his mother's new cause, he was forced to regard her in another light. All that silly makeup. On the whole, he liked the Jenny Option, as he dubbed it—the master and the little governess, though of course he was not so old.

Emilio's eyes were closed. Tom tugged on his hair. They opened. "Am I handsome?" the older man asked. "Bel visage?" Emilio smiled and kissed his hand. "Si, signore. Very bel." He closed his eyes again.

Tom thought how much fun it would be, shopping with her, fixing that alarming hair. But maybe she would not be fixed. He thought fondly of the metallic smile that she could summon at will. Maybe she would not be fixed. He had always thought it entirely likely that she was wanted by the Connecticut police. He finished his wine, and kissed Emilio gently on the mouth.

"You will have to go home soon," he said softly.

"Si, signore."

"Back home to Napoli," he elaborated.

"Si."

Emilio opened his sorrowful eyes and put his arm around Tom's neck.

ANTOINETTE KOVALENKO, WITH JENNY IN TOW, APPEARED ON the doorstep at Gramercy Park at eight o'clock precisely. Tom let them in, and beamed at the old woman. "Mrs.

III P I R A T E J E N N Y III

Kovalenko! And Jenny. So good of you to come. Mother's been looking forward to it all day." He took Antoinette's arm and walked her to the room where his mother sat. Jenny followed, expressionless.

"Mrs. Claverack." Jenny shook her hand. Tom watched her as she backed into a chair and sat like an army private. Not clumsy at all, he thought.

They sipped sweet vermouth, as nothing else was offered. Antoinette was clearly uneasy, but she loosened up under the thank-yous for her help with the benefit, and launched a story about a party in the Adirondacks with accompanying hand gestures. Tom looked at Jenny and left the room.

"Excuse me," he heard her say, as she followed.

"What is going on?" she hissed in the hallway. "Why are we here?"

"You are meeting my mother," he said, and kissed her very suddenly, before she could answer. Then he pushed her back into the sitting room.

Dinner was roast beef, baked potatoes, peas, and sour red wine. Jenny drank three glasses, and wondered if she would have to use the passports very soon. She felt exactly like a rabbit being hunted. Tom drank water. Mrs. Kovalenko and Mrs. Claverack swapped museum stories. Dessert, strawberry shortcake, was followed by weak coffee.

Tom stood up and kissed his mother on the cheek. "Jenny and I are going to go for a short walk," he said. "We'll be right back."

Passive as a lamb, the girl allowed him to fit her into her coat. He walked quickly out the door, and she had to skip to keep up with him, down the sidewalk and up to the park gate, which he opened with his key. She followed him onto the well-groomed gravel path. The night was chilly, and there was no one else about. He took her elbow and steered her to a bench. Her face was as blank as a piece of paper in the light of the street lamp. He rubbed his face against the nape of her neck. She did not stir.

"What are you doing," she asked, not coquettishly.

"I am kissing your neck," he replied.

"What am I doing here?" she asked, firmly, and he sighed and desisted.

"This," he drawled, "is social life. Parties, dinners, obligations, and pleasures. What do you think?"

"I think?" The girl narrowed her eyes. "I think I smell a rat."

"Excellent use of the American idiom," he said, and kissed her until she responded. "You're a lot of work," he observed, while she caught her breath. "But I think we should get married."

Jenny stood up abruptly. "Oh please," she sneered.

"I'm quite serious," said Tom, in an I'm-quite-serious voice. "Mother would be so pleased. And you'd like it."

"I don't think you're at all funny," said Jenny. She walked toward the gate.

Tom stamped his feet in the cold, like a horse, and laughed. "But I've got a ring, and everything," he complained. He stuck his hand in his coat pocket and pulled out a box. He held it out to Jenny and was rewarded by the sight of her moving slowly back into the light.

"Your hair is ridiculous," he said.

"That's not very romantic," she said, and she took the box. Inside was a bright, pale stone.

"It's a yellow diamond," explained Tom. "Put it on."

The ring was too big for any of her fingers except the index. The stone was vast. "We can have it sized. It's more than four carats. What do you say?"

"Is this real?"

"Ask your Netta."

"Why do you want to *marry* me?"

"Because, as I told you before, I like to do many, many things, and I think you would like to do them with me."

"Can I think about it?"

He kissed her and bit her lips and sucked the blood. She pushed away. Her eyes were wet.

"Could you just stop this?" she demanded.

"No, I don't think so," he said, and he put his hands inside her coat. She kissed him. After a minute, he pulled away.

"You think about it," he said. "Give me back the ring while you're thinking." He unlocked the gate and they walked in silence to his mother's house.

Two days later, she called. She said she had thought about it and discussed it with Netta and Nikki and they had called Mrs. Claverack and everyone thought it would be all right. But she had a condition. Tom asked what it was. She wanted to go to Germany for the honeymoon. He said that would be easy, and asked her to set the date. She told him to do it. He said in two weeks. She said fine. And—oh. They would have to see a lawyer for a prenuptial contract. Mrs. Claverack had talked to Nikki about the whole thing.

Tom hung up the phone, rolled over, and told Carlos to call a car for him in the morning.

16

IT WAS ALL TOO EASY. THE CONVE-
nience of the exit: from the Kovalenkos', New York, the
United States. She was bothered by the public nature of the
exodus—that, and the lingering whiff of rodent. After all,
the only thing she was really afraid of was Tom. Well, and
Bart. And Isolde. And Fritz. But Tom seemed to want to be
on her side. Could she play on a team? She doubted it.

It was not hard to reason that he must have an ulterior
motive for marrying her. She suspected the mother, and
therefore suspected the money. Weren't some trust funds
dependent on certain conditions? Did he need an heir?
This sounded so old-fashioned. There was no one to ask;

but she knew she would not be allowed near the money, and therefore she felt safe.

They saw the lawyer, who inhabited an eyrie in the GM Building. He was a white-haired man with a jolly mouth and chin and the eyes of a serial killer. The agreement entitled Jenny to a pitiful sum of money, with slight increments over the years, should the marriage dissolve for any reason whatsoever. Several pieces of family jewelry were also settled upon her outright, for her perpetual use and the use of her heirs thereafter.

"You got rooked," Tom remarked to her in the elevator.

"Did I?" said Jenny, and tried to look worried.

Netta continually wavered between distress at losing Jenny and a thrilled, not very complimentary, awe at the match. One day, Jenny saw her shuffling through her papers. When asked what she was looking for, Netta mumbled something vague. Jenny quickly extracted the paper with the safe combination from where she had tucked it in the seam of a drawer, and shuffled it into the pile. A moment later, paper in hand, Netta scuttled to the elevator.

They shopped for a modest trousseau. They found a dress, and some underwear, but beyond that, Netta was astonished that what Jenny really wanted was two pairs of colored contact lenses—one green, one violet. And a leather zippered portfolio case.

"Maybe I will become an artist, after all," Jenny laughed, by way of explanation. Netta fussed and gave to Jenny many of the same articles of clothing the girl had already inhabited over the summer months.

They were to be married on Saturday, November 7. On Tuesday, Jenny and Tom met with Peter Montayne in his church offices for a premarital counseling session. Montayne, a short man with thinning, strawberry-blond hair aloft and a neatly trimmed red beard below, was awkwardly hearty in the presence of Thomas Claverack. Tom extended his hand like a piece of marble statuary, and Peter's damp paw slid from it, then bedewed Jenny's palm.

"This is quite an occasion," the minister said. "I hope you won't mind, but, uh, there are certain guidelines issued by the central church committee—from the Boston crowd, you know them, Tom!—and I feel we must follow them in this, as in all other cases of prospective marriage that come into my—my jurisdiction."

"A minister's gotta do what a minister's gotta do," said Tom, smiling, and linked his arm through Jenny's.

Peter fumbled about on the table. He picked up two forms and two small pencils, the kind with no erasers. "We've found—"he rattled a pint or so of mucus about in his throat—"that, well, these standardized personality tests can be helpful as"—he gurgled—"as a means of opening discussion on relevant personal and, uh, spiritual matters. So if you could both just uh, sit down, and take a few moments—" Tom helped Jenny off with her coat, removed his, and laid them carefully along the back of the couch. He and Jenny sat side by side and leaned over the coffee table, filling in boxes in answer to multiple-choice questions.

"When I disagree with someone about a matter of personal taste, I (1) Leave the room; (2) Engage him in a thoughtful discussion of the subject; (3) Start an argument; (4) Consult an objective third party."

"When I go to sleep at night, I most often feel (1) Restless and anxious; (2) Depressed; (3) Satisfied and at peace; (4) Nothing at all; I just feel sleepy."

While the reverend retired to the bathroom and made

strangled sinus noises, Jenny and Tom briskly filled out the forms. The final question was:

"Concerning the education of my children, I plan (1) To raise them as churchgoing Christians in the Unitarian Universalist Church; (2) To read them the Bible at home and allow them to make their own decisions about religion when they are older; (3) To refrain from all religious training; (4) Other."

Jenny carefully blackened in the box beside number 1, and, glancing at Tom's, saw that he had done the same. He caught her eye, then quickly handed the forms to the minister.

For the next few minutes, while Tom cracked his knuckles and stretched and Jenny practiced her perfect sitting posture, Peter collated their answers and transferred them to a graph, then found a ruler and connected the dots. He looked up smiling.

"Well! Well! Look at this!" He held up the graph, on which two nearly horizontal lines ran closely parallel or overlapping. He read from the literature: "You are both 'happy and industrious, with excellent interpersonal skills and a well-developed spiritual and moral structure.' You are well suited to one another."

"Yes, I know, said Tom, and he looked into Jenny's eyes. Suddenly her vision contracted to a point, as in the glaucoma test, and her mind went black with desire.

"Now," said Peter, "the service itself, though simple, is profound. . . ." Jenny controlled her breathing with enormous effort, but could not hear what the man was saying.

The night before her wedding, Jenny went up to visit with Nikki. He told her that he had not changed his mind; he would not give her away. He told her that she was ungrateful, a gold-digger, and that she had made a bad deal in the bargain. "All in all," he concluded, "you've been quite a waste of time." He switched the television on.

When the house was dark, Jenny tiptoed up to the desk in the gallery. She found the lock combination and recopied the numbers, inaccurately, onto another slip of paper, which she distressed and returned to the pile. With the right combination in her hand, she stealthily climbed to Nikki's lair and very, very carefully pulled out the television and opened the safe. She removed more than half the contents, and closed it again. Then she went back to her room, stuffed the jewelry into a cosmetics bag, and burned the combination. She put the cosmetics bag in her carryall; her trunk, an old battered thing, was already locked. She lay down on her bed and put on her earphones. All of the music sounded different now, even clearer than before, as if she had said the words first. They came from her mouth. And she had a new tape: Weill's *Der Ozeanflug*—Lindbergh's Flight. She was really going to be flying, well, sailing, to Europe herself, and the music stirred her strangely. Those thundering sounds, all the strings in the orchestra and the drums, with the sound of the chorus, like a possessed church choir, demonic, shouting to chords that were dischords, and Jenny imagined the ocean rolling, the clouds breaking, she foresaw the heroism of her voyage. It was dark and triumphant, and she would never come back.

In the hush of a misty Saturday morning, at nine o'clock, Jenny walked alone down the aisle of the First Unitarian Universalist Church. She wore a waltz-length dress of ivory-colored Irish linen and lace, with a standing collar. Her hair was combed up in the back and rolled up in front, and a spray of lily-of-the-valley was anchored to one side of the roll. In her hands she carried Netta's prayer book. As she walked slowly, to the minor-key flutter from the organist, she looked like a doll without a mouth; in honor of the occasion, she had forgone lipstick. But her eyes were dark as a raccoon's.

Netta, with Mrs. Hayworth as escort, sat on the edge of the left front pew. Mrs. Claverack stood beside her cousin, John Battersby, who was also the executor of Mr. Claverack's estate. There were no attendants, and Montayne skipped the "Who gives this woman?" line.

Tom half-smiled while the minister droned the familiar words; Jenny looked chastened, almost grim. They did not look at one another as they exchanged vows. Tom did not receive a ring, but he put the yellow diamond on Jenny's finger. It caught all the lights in the church—a gaudy, Catholic thing. The minister told Tom he could kiss the bride. He leaned over and planted his lips on Jenny's forehead, as if in benediction. A wave of unease rippled through the church, then dissipated in the swelling organ exeunt.

They filed into cars and drove uptown to the Kovalenkos, where Elizabeth and Keaton, cheering, met them at the door. They had blown up white balloons and draped them, tied with white crepe paper, about the dining room. Mrs. Hayworth's wedding breakfast was her best effort: cheese and raspberry blintzes and white sausages and apple butter. Two bottles of champagne were consumed and the couple's health drunk, but no one made any speeches except Tom, who stood and said simply: "My lovely bride—Jenny Freuhoffer Claverack."

Mrs. Claverack gave Jenny a circlet brooch of pearls and diamonds—one of the items specified in the prenuptial contract—and Jenny arranged her face into a look of surprise and pleasure. Netta gave her a present from her and Nikki, a stickpin crowned with the golden head of a heron, sporting a tiny sapphire eye. Elizabeth cooed. Spiderman ate three lengths of white sausage and got sick on the stair carpet. Keaton was blamed, and exited crying to his room. Nikolai Nikolaievich did not come downstairs.

Mrs. Claverack and Mr. Battersby left with Tom, who would be back to fetch Jenny. The *Queen Christina* sailed at three P.M. Jenny's trunk was already down at the pier.

"Netta?" said Jenny, after she had changed out of her dress and into her traveling costume, a blue angora sweater and a kilt. Netta had just wakened from a short champagne-induced nap. Nikki was still upstairs. Elizabeth, Mrs. Hayworth, and Keaton had gone to the park.

"Yes, dear?" said Netta, smiling like a mother frog.

"I want the painting in your bedroom."

"The German?"

"Yes. Please give it to me."

Netta looked distressed. "Jenny, that is not very nice. You cannot have the *painting.*"

"You said yourself that no one has ever heard of Auermann."

"That's not the point."

"I would like to have it."

Netta frowned. "You are very excited. A bride can do no wrong, but you—you are being naughty! Stop it."

Jenny looked at her hands, and spoke softly. "I know about Mrs. Spencer and the museum in St. Paul." Netta looked uncomprehending for a moment.

"You read my mail!"

"Yes. And I talked with Mrs. Spencer, several times. Does anyone else know about your plan to dispose of the paintings? Does Nikki?"

"Of course he knows."

"No, I bet not. And wouldn't Nicholas be just a little

upset, to learn that his mother did *not* plan to leave him her glorious collection, but preferred to give it away to a museum in the Midwest because of personal vanity?"

"Carla would sell them!"

Jenny looked at her. "I could ask for a lot more," she said. "But I just want 'The Seasons.' "

Netta clasped her hands and brought them to her breast, which she then pounded. "You! I gave you my home, my things! I loved you! You are a wretch, and a *peasant* and a thief!"

"I am sorry. Give me the painting."

Netta fetched a pair of shears from the kitchen. As Jenny followed silently behind, she rode the elevator up to the third floor. In her bedroom—where wedding clothes were strewn about on all the surfaces—she went up to the painting and snipped the trip wire that led to the alarm system. Then she dropped the shears on the floor and left the room.

Jenny lifted the painting off the wall. She worked the backing tape off, and pulled it out of its ornate gilt frame. She wrapped the painted panel in a pink-and-yellow baby blanket, then packed it into her leather portfolio. It fit snugly. The photo of Lotte Lenya and Kurt Weill was slipped into the inside pocket. She zipped it up, and lugged it downstairs to the foyer. There she stood and watched through the lace curtains for Tom's car.

17

JENNY SWUNG THE KEY ON HER FINGER and looked about the small cabin. "I thought you said we were first class."

"This is first class. This is a boat."

"It does not look like a movie." Jenny dropped her bag, and sat on the edge of the bed. Tom sat beside her and picked up her left hand, which lay limp, glittering, in his. Jenny was deadpan.

"You are a rag doll," he said, and bounced her hand, which flapped obligingly. "Is this a—tactic?"

Jenny turned her innocent face towards his. Her eyes were very yellow, like her diamond.

"Shall we observe the departure?" he inquired.

III PIRATE JENNY III

"Fine."

They climbed to the upper deck, where a few passengers, the very young and the old, stood, red-nosed in the cold, waving hankies to those on the pier. The whistle blew. Jenny jumped a foot, and Tom laughed.

They toured the ballroom, the game room, and the dining rooms, all empty. They sat in a bar and Tom ordered a cognac for Jenny and a ginger ale for himself. He avoided touching her. He hailed an older couple to join them at their booth, and introduced Jenny, dismissively, as "my wife." They talked about the boat. About other boats. About the crossing. About Arlington, Virginia, where the couple came from. About Hamburg, where in five days the boat would dock, and where they had never been. About New York. Jenny stood up.

"I have to go back to the cabin. I'll see you later."

Alone in the room, she glanced out the porthole at the receding skyline of New York City. It looked shiny from this distance, almost the grand and pretty toy she had once imagined cities to be. She unlocked her trunk and fingered the contents listlessly. She put a few things in the dresser, then pinned up her hair and took off her clothes. She took a hot shower that lasted a long time. Upon emerging, she raised a cloud of iris-scented talcum about herself and redrew her eyes. Then she donned a peignoir—a black, beribboned thing. Netta had been distressed by her color choice.

She poured another cognac from the little bar next to the fridge, unwrapped her painting, and propped it up on the low dresser. She sat down in an easy chair and regarded her trophy. How merry the lovers looked, under the tree! How sweetly smiled the mother at her son, how fearfully did the old man regard the wintry sky. It seemed to her that the world contained in the painting spun around, faster and faster, sucking her into the middle, to a still point. She shook her head and looked away. She knew that she could not leap from the spinning world. But she considered how she might jump from one tree to another, and then back. The seasons, after all, repeated indefinitely. Didn't they? She sipped the cognac.

A while later, Tom came into the cabin, and barely looked at her. "Phew! What a smell! Do you use cheap perfume, too?"

"It's dusting powder."

"Hey, what's this? Is it from the Kovalenkos?"

"Yes. It's Netta's special wedding present to me."

He looked at the painting. "And you brought it along on the trip?"

"I like to look at it."

"No accounting for tastes, as my mother often says." He seemed to register her for the first time. "What are you wearing? There's a cocktail reception in half an hour. Don't you want to come along?"

"No," said Jenny, and drank.

"Oh? What do you want?"

"I want you to come here."

He walked slowly to the chair. "Yes?"

Jenny smiled icily. "You know, you are forgetting something."

"I forget nothing."

"We were married this morning."

"I remember that."

Jenny stood and walked behind Tom. She tugged at his jacket shoulders and slipped the jacket down over his arms. He stood still. One at a time, she disengaged his arms. She dropped the coat onto the chair. She stood before him, very close, and lifted her hands as if to touch him, but held them instead an inch from his chest. She looked like a supplicant, as she smiled into his dark brown eyes. He did not smile.

"A marriage," she said, as though in conversation at the cocktail reception, "should be consummated, I've always heard."

"Is that what you would like?" he asked, politely.

"That is what I would like."

"Unbutton my shirt."

Tom and Jenny stayed in the cabin for a day and a half. During that time, Jenny's wishes were often consulted—and, just as often, they were not.

The morning of the 9th, they sat on pillows on the floor and ate a load of scrambled eggs, bacon, and coffee and watched a news program on the closed circuit.

"It's November ninth!" exclaimed Jenny. "My birthday!" She was nineteen.

"Yes," said Tom. "I'm sure you'll forgive the observation that you don't look anywhere near twenty-three, which is what I calculate from your passport you are."

"I'm almost twenty years younger than you," said Jenny, with a mouth full of bacon. "You, on the other hand, look your age." She leaned over and tickled the inside of his thigh, in apology for the insult.

"Can I have my passport back, by the way?" she asked, an hour later.

"I thought I'd look after our papers." He put on a robe and walked into the bathroom, shouting over the sound of his pissing, "Where did you get it, anyway?"

Jenny sat up. "What?"

"The passport."

"Germany, of course. Berlin."

Tom stood in the doorway. "Spare us," he said. His beard was a dark shadow on his face and neck, and he ran a hand through his silky dark hair, reciting theatrically:

> *"Frisch weht der Wind*
> *der Heimat zu:*
> *mein irisch Kind,*
> *wo weilest du?*
> *Sind's deiner Seufer Wehen,*
> *die mir die Segel blahen?*
> *Wehe, wehe, du Wind!*
> *Weh, ach weh, mein Kind!"*

Jenny stared at him.

"You see?" he said. "I knew you didn't know German."

"It's your accent," said Jenny. "It's appalling."

Tom laughed and turned on the shower.

They ventured out around noon. The weather was cold and whipped at them along the walkways. Tom took Jenny into the mall of diminutive shops on the third below-decks, left her looking at a showcase of hats while he went into the drugstore, and came out carrying a package, mysteriously claiming that it was her birthday present. Now matter how she teased, he would not show it, but kept the bag tucked securely in his jacket pocket.

A pianist, a guitarist, and a bongo player shared a disco beat in the Continental Lounge. A handsome blond Danish boy brought their drinks. Later, at lunch, smiles were exchanged among the other inhabitants of their table in reference to the couple's previous absence. A toast was raised to "the newlyweds."

"How do they know?" whispered Jenny.

"I told the ship when I made the reservations. That's how we got such a *tiny* stateroom."

A French family was part of their table, and Tom chatted with them in their language. There was a daughter, about eight, and a son, about fourteen. Both children had dark hair and striking blue eyes. Tom asked the boy a lot of questions about his school—at least, so Jenny guessed. She felt something intangible, cold, like ice water, lapping at her toes.

When they returned to their room after lunch, Jenny lit a joint.

Tom frowned. "I didn't know you smoked that stuff," he said. "Don't you want to see your present?"

"Yes," said Jenny, and held out her hand.

Tom unwrapped it for her. It was a white glass jar of French cold cream.

"What's that for?"

Tom grabbed her arm and steered her into the bathroom. "Remove the eye makeup," he commanded.

"Why?"

"Because it's too much. You look like a fortune-teller."

"I like it."

"Wipe it off. Couldn't someone in the beauty shop show you how to apply makeup properly? I can't be expected to know everything."

Jenny took a tissue and daubed the white stuff over one eye. It stung. She wiped. Tom stood close behind her, watching.

"You like boys," she said, suddenly.

Tom smiled. "Ah," he said.

Jenny looked at him in the mirror.

"As I said," he said, "I like many, many things."

She had cold-cream streaks over one eye; the other was still dark. He put his hands at her waist, pinning her arms at her sides. "I know," she said.

Before dinner, Tom took Jenny to the ship's beauty parlor and asked them to do something with her hair. They cut it and feathered it and blew it dry, then stripped it, gooed it, and highlighted it. They brushed a touch of mascara on her lashes, and found a darling tea-rose shade for her lips and cheeks. When they were done, her hair, brushed back from her face, was brown with blondish streaks, and her face was flushed. She was not in a good mood, and her ill temper was exacerbated by dinner, where the couples at the table (the Manhoffs, the Fleuries, the Samuelsons) told her how lovely she looked. Eventually, she tuned them out, pasting onto her face the look of calm, august pleasure she had learned from Tom. And her mind ran away, top speed, bringing her back picture after picture: the duelist who stabs his opponent through the heart; the lion who with one lash of his tail breaks open the cage door; the woman straitjacketed in the mental institution who, after days of concentration, wills her limbs to limpness and slips loose from the bindings—see how she runs from the asylum, across the broad green lawn cluttered with wheelchairs, into the woods where spring has touched the trees with pale green buds, tiny knives of life!

Back in their room, Tom told her how he would take her shopping in Hamburg, in Cologne, in Vienna, in Milan, in Paris. How much she would enjoy that. Jenny pulled out her makeup and went to work on her face in the bathroom.

"Stop that!" Tom shouted.

He slapped the eyeliner out of her hand, and it drew a

haiku in the sink. "You're going to stop looking like a tramp! Davey Potter may like the slutty look, but you are married to me now, and you have to straighten up."

"How the fuck would you know what David Potter likes? You don't even know him."

Tom smiled. "Oh yes, I do," he said. "But let's be precise. I *used* to know him—quite well."

JENNY WENT SWIMMING IN THE POOL THAT NIGHT. SHE WAS alone, so she switched off the pool-room lights and swam by the underwater lamps, and by the light of the nearly full moon that shone through the glass wall and ceiling. The sea outside had gotten rough, and the clouds moved about the moon, so that its light was a flicker.

Because the pool water was salt, Jenny felt very buoyant, almost as if she were slithering along on top of the water. She swam a few laps, then floated on her back and stared at the moon. When the ship listed, she could actually see the waves below. My tears, she thought, and the salt pool and the salty ocean, all salt. She thought of Lot's wife and couldn't remember the point of the story. She rolled over and swam, thinking. She thought about Houdini, about weights and ropes, about wrists in handcuffs, about how if you made your hand tiny like a bird, it could flutter through the ring of metal and fly away. Where would it fly? She thought about what she called Zen: disentanglement, flight from a dark house, the feel of peach silk on her skin, the smell of roses, heavy soft pillows. She thought so hard she forgot how long she'd been in, and was almost sleeping on top of the water, her breaths like snores, her strokes like rocking. She shook herself and climbed out.

Though it was late, the pharmacy was still open, and

there Jenny charged several things. She returned to the room, which was empty, and paced. The wild sadness of Lenya's voice whispered through the room, under the roar of the sea:

> *But I've been walking through the night and the day*
> *Till my eyes get weary and my hair turns to grey*
> *And sometimes I think maybe God's gone away,*
> *Forgetting the promise that he made that day—*
> *And we're lost out here in the stars. . . .*

Tom came in late, moving unsteadily. He smelled bad; he had been drinking.

"It's too bright," he said, and turned off the light. He lurched toward Jenny and hauled her to the porthole. The moon moved on her face.

"Is your face clean?"

"It's completely clean." She tried to kiss him, but he held his left hand at her throat and opened her robe with his right. He bit her shoulders and her neck, he bit her breasts, in short, hard snaps, and dragged her to the bed, where he fell on her, biting. Very shortly he was asleep, his face wedged between her thighs, his teeth tangled in her hair. She pushed him away and went into the bathroom. The skin was broken in only a few places, but there would be many bruises. She ran a bath, and sat in the tub, scrubbing her body, anger drying the tears before they could fall. She amended her plans, slightly.

Early in the morning, Jenny wandered through the dining room, laid out with orange and yellow juice pitchers and napkin tents, until she found the kitchen. In one room, the dishwashers, wreathed in steam, stacked plates from the bin.

lll   PIRATE JENNY   lll

"I would like to buy a knife," she said softly.

The Caribbean man spoke English. He picked up a butter knife from the cutlery basket and handed it to her. "No charge," he said, and smiled.

"No, no," said Jenny. A sharp knife."

"A steak knife?"

"A chopping knife," she said, and pointed to the rack of gleaming blades above the stove.

"How much money you got? Fifty?"

Jenny drew a twenty-dollar bill out of her pocket. "That's all," she said.

He shrugged and disappeared into a further room, where he spoke in Spanish and she heard a couple of voices laugh, and dispute. He returned with an object in his hand.

"Switchblade," he said, and pushed the button, showing her. The blade was thin and rusted. Jenny gave him the bill, took the knife, and left the kitchen.

She sat at her table and drank several glasses of grapefruit juice. The knife was heavy in her sweater pocket. She had the waiter make a bloody mary, which she carried back to the room. Tom was up, sitting in a chair in his underwear, looking old. She smiled and handed him the drink. Perched on the arm of the chair, she leaned over and rubbed his sandpaper chin.

"It's our last day on the boat," she said. "Take me shopping."

That afternoon, Tom bought her an evening dress, blue satin with a ring of blue stones sewn into the neck. The clerk pretended not to notice the blue-and-yellow mottlings on Jenny's shoulders. Jenny looked about forty-five in the dress, but she squeaked with pleasure and persuaded Tom to buy her, also, a pair of black silk pants, a full white cotton blouse, and a wide brown belt. In the shoe boutique, they found a pair of pink marabou mules, conservative tennis sneakers, black satin pumps, and, because Jenny begged so prettily, a pair of short black boots with pointed toes.

Modeling the clothes in the room took a few hours. Then Jenny said, "Let's do something really decadent."

Tom sneered slightly. "Whatever can you mean?"

"I'm going to order only decadent food, and we have to eat it *all.*"

"Like the Grande Bouffe?"

"Like a Roman pig-out."

The tray rolled in: caviar and mashed potatoes and ice cream sundaes and milk shakes and champagne and fried onion rings and prosciutto on crackers and eggs benedict and jam crêpes and lemonade. Jenny fed Tom ice cream, and he smeared caviar on her breasts and nibbled it off grain by grain.

Tom drank half his chocolate milk shake, and laughed. "Not since I was a kid!"

"You have to finish it."

But Tom stood up and danced instead, a solo waltz, then fell on the bed, laughing. Jenny watched him, worried. Had he drunk enough? The entire contents of a package of nonprescription sleeping pills, ground up, plus half a bottle, at least, of liquid orange-flavor Valium. She wondered if it might kill him. Tom was out.

Still smeared with food, Jenny stripped entirely and went into the bathroom. She took a razor to her head and removed most of her hair and then foamed in some black dye. She sat on the toilet seat for the designated twenty minutes. Then she showered and the excess ran like ink over her body.

She dressed in her black pants and boots and her new blouse. It was one A.M. She extracted a key from Tom's pants pocket. He was still breathing. She tied a green scarf over her head, did her makeup hurriedly, and went in search of an officer. In the Lieder Lounge, the purser was dancing with a short, pretty woman.

"I'm so sorry to bother you," said Jenny breathlessly. "But I need to get our things. Tom's such a planner—he's packing everything now. Do you mind?" She smiled.

The purser sighed but excused himself from his partner and led the way.

"Have you ever been married?" Jenny asked, tremulously.

"Once," he said. "For a few years."

"It's all new to me," she said, and smiled bravely. "Sometimes he's just very hard to—to *please,* you know?"

The purser, who was thirty-five, looked at her pointedly. "Maybe you should have married someone your own age," he said, as he opened the door to the security office.

"Oh," giggled Jenny, "I think you're flirting with me." She handed him the key, and from the safety deposit box he retrieved their passports, traveler's checks, cash, and her Claverack jewelry. She put everything in her handbag.

"I have to get back," she said, regretfully. "Tom will get mad."

Tom was still out cold. Into her carryall she stuffed the Kovalenko stash bag (where her French passport was also secreted), the Claverack stash, her German passport, and the cash—which was only five hundred dollars. She thought a moment and took Tom's passport, too. She said a silent farewell to most of her clothes, stuffing only her peignoir, a sweater, her tennis shoes, a beret, and a stack of silk scarves into the bag. She did not forget her tapes and recorder.

They would dock in Hamburg at six. She put on Tom's black leather trench coat; the sleeves were too long. She took a razor blade and sliced off about four inches of cuff. The belt she discarded and replaced with her new brown one, which cinched tightly at the waist. She removed the ribbon from Tom's gray fedora and replaced it with a pink satin tie from a teddy she left behind, and planted the hat over the green scarf on her head. She dragged the portfolio and the carryall to the door and set them down. Then she opened the knife and sat in the chair.

Tom was still asleep, but snoring now. His watch was old, so the dial no longer glowed. Jenny fastened it to her wrist and went into the bathroom to read the dial. It was after four.

She left the room.

III P I R A T E J E N N Y III

18

PEOPLE AND LUGGAGE THUMPED IN the passageway. That, and the stillness of the ship, woke him. He was wearing a pair of pants and his socks. The room smelled foul and nausea struck him in the gut. His head was in pain. All of him was in pain, but not awake, as he stumbled over dishes and bottles and food to the bathroom and was sick with diarrhea. There were purple-gray stains in the bathtub. Where was his watch? What time was it?

Barely awake, and very ill, he pulled on a shirt and some slippers. The traveler's checks were on the dresser. How had they gotten there? He registered that Jenny was gone.

The passageway was crowded with people laughing and

shouting at their children and with porters hauling luggage in carts. He somehow struggled through and squeezed onto the elevator that went up. There was a bottleneck at the head of the gangplank, where the customs official bantered with the passengers. He made his way to the rail, and saw a figure stepping onto the dock below. For a moment, he hallucinated that he saw himself, in his trench coat and fedora, only as a young man.

"Jenny?" he said in a conversational tone. "Jenny!" he screamed. He realized he did not know her name.

She was tugging on the portfolio in one hand and had the carryall in the other. Before her rose the brown-and-gray city, swathed in fog and drizzle—white smoke belching here, twin cathedral spires fuzzily outlined there, and yellow and green and red lights flashing.

She ran a few steps, and caught up with a couple that had just come off another boat. Her dark red mouth moved—he could see it all the way from the deck. What was she saying? He strained, and tilted his head, as if he could hear, in the roar of the departing crowds and the boat sirens and the heavy chains rattling and the engines in the hold. What was she saying?

"I'm so sorry to bother you, but I don't speak a word of German, and I've lost my way. Can you help me?"

The man took her portfolio and the woman took her arm. He saw her smile, and the trio walked towards the taxi stand. The ship's railing was very cold. He squinted and then he lost the black car in the fog, in the drizzle, in the maze of lights and shadows, as she vanished into the bosom of her homeland.